MISTLETOE & CHAIN MAIL

HOLIDAY KNIGHTS SERIES - BOOK 1 - CHRISTMAS

ELIZABETH ROSE

ROSESCRIBE MEDIA INC.

CHAPTER 1

THE CHRISTMAS GOOSE

14TH CENTURY ENGLAND, CHRISTMAS EVE

*H*is goose was cooked and there was no turning back now! If Sir Adam de Ware couldn't complete this latest secret assignment for King Edward III, then there was no hope of ever becoming a baron.

"Sir Adam, is this really necessary? After all, it is Christmas Eve," his squire reminded him as they climbed the stairs of the great hall of Cavendish Castle in Sudbury. His squire held Adam's secret weapon with two hands, balancing the covered gift that was going to be his ticket to get inside the castle.

"Bryce, I don't need you telling me things I already know," said Adam, surveying the lords and ladies that crowded the landing. It was a cold day in December and a light dusting of snow covered the ground. The castle courtyard was decorated for the occasion with fir boughs wrapped around tall poles that were topped off with lit torches. This served as a lined entranceway leading to the keep for those arriving for the festivities.

"But we haven't been invited to the celebration," Bryce pointed out. "We don't even know Earl Cavendish, and I've only seen his daughter once in passing. As soon as the guards discover that we've snuck in without an invitation, they will throw us out."

"Keep quiet." Adam scanned the area, noticing a drunken soldier leaning over the well in the courtyard, retching. A woman who seemed to be the castle's whore giggled and entertained two men at once in the shadows of the mews. Another woman with a young boy stopped in her tracks as the whore lifted the hem of her gown. Covering the boy's eyes with her hand, she yanked her son in the opposite direction and hurried away.

Cheerful music floated in the air and the smell of mutton, braised leeks, and roasted goose made his stomach grumble. He looked over his shoulder, scowling at Bryce who was watching a serving wench instead of where he was going. He tripped, but managed to quickly right himself and not drop the gift Adam brought for Lady Eva.

"God's eyes, be careful, Squire!" Adam reprimanded the boy. "If that falls, I'll have your head. I didn't spend the last two hours basting that prized goose over an open fire in the freezing cold to have you spill it at the witch's doorstep."

Bryce looked up at Adam and his eyes opened wide like a deer in the torchlight. "Lady Eva," he whispered.

"Aye, I'm talking about Lady Eva. Of course, I am. You know she's said to be the stuffiest lady in all of Christendom. I've heard she has such a cold heart that her simple gaze can freeze a man's blood, not unlike the gorgon, Medusa."

"M – my lord," said Bryce, mumbling as always. Adam continued talking.

"I've heard the woman never smiles and even at the age of five and twenty, no man has ever agreed to marry her." He chuckled lowly. "She'd be an asset on the battlefield since most men would probably run in fear when they saw her."

"My lord," said Bryce again, making a face and looking very uncomfortable. But Adam paid him no mind.

"Quit your mumbling, Squire. I'll admit, I've never seen this Lady Eva. But from the stories told by the bards, I swear she must look like a cross between a dog and a wild boar."

"But, my lord!" Bryce jerked his head upward a few times and rolled his eyes, looking like he was having a convulsion.

"Squire, stop acting like a fool! You tend to be too clumsy, and I won't have that. Not tonight," said Adam with a shake of his head.

Bryce jerked his head again and cleared his throat. The boy was always acting like a court jester and this wasn't the time for it.

"A spoiled goose will do naught to thaw the cold heart of the ice princess," said Adam with another chuckle. "I can only hope she likes hot meat because, mayhap, then I can melt the icicles that –"

Adam stopped short when he saw someone's reflection on the outside of the metal lid covering the goose.

"She's standing right behind me, isn't she?" he mumbled, feeling the knot in his stomach twisting so hard that his throat became tight. He felt as if he were about to choke.

"What is the meaning of this?" snapped a woman from behind him. "I will not have my name mentioned in such a dishonorable way."

Adam slowly turned around, surprised to see the most beautiful woman he'd ever laid eyes on in his life. Surely, there had to be some mistake. This couldn't be the wicked Lady of Cavendish. She looked far too fair and beautiful. Her long, oaken hair was worn loose and covered with a jeweled metal circlet with a small, thin veil attached. Her angry eyes, the color of weathered acorns, scrutinized him, causing a shiver to run up his spine by the intensity of her glare. She wore no cloak, but her burgundy velvet gown with long, green silk tippets covered her completely and looked very warm. The woman wasn't thin, but then again, neither was she fat. In Adam's opinion, she had just the right amount of sensuous curves to make her enticing.

"Lady Eva, I presume?" Part of him hoped it was she and another part wished it wasn't after what he'd just said about her with him not knowing she was listening.

"Aye, I am Lady Eva Cavendish, daughter of the earl. Who are you, knave?"

Adam flinched inwardly when she called him knave since it was a low blow to refer to any knight in such a derogative manner. Still, he supposed he deserved it after his poor behavior on her doorstep. Damn, he should have been more careful. He might have just blown the whole mission with his loose tongue.

"I am Sir Adam de Ware, at your service." He got down on one knee and reached up to kiss her hand, but she did nothing to offer it to him. Instead, she held her hands balled up in fists, glaring at him as if she hated him even though she had just met him.

"I don't believe I know you," she said in a clipped tone. "And I also don't recall your name being on the guest list. I am aware of every person who has been invited, and you are not one of them. Guard!" she called out, raising her hand to flag over a soldier in the courtyard.

Adam's chin snapped upward. He had to do something fast! If he didn't get invited to this celebration, he might just as well kiss his opportunity goodbye of being granted the title of baron. After five long years of taking on special assignments from the king as his personal spy, Adam felt he deserved to be called Baron. He'd taken many risks and worked too hard to let the shrew ruin his chances now. Nay, he had to quickly think of another approach.

"The Bishop of Sudbury sent me," he blurted out, getting up and brushing the snow off his knee.

The woman wrinkled her nose as if she didn't believe

him. "Why would the bishop send a scoundrel like you to my doorstep?"

That dug into him like a knife. "It was his wish I bring this gift to the earl as gratitude for all he does for the church." Adam was counting on the fact that the earl even knew the bishop. It was a chance he had to take. "And I must add that it's not polite to call me a scoundrel when you've just met me, my lady."

"And I suppose it's in good form to be insulting the hostess behind her back right on her own doorstep?" She had a point there. Adam squeezed his eyes closed, cursing himself inwardly for his stupid mistake. "Guard, throw these men out of here at once," she commanded.

"Nay," pleaded Adam, holding his palms forward as the guard stomped up the stairs to get them. "I'm sorry, my lady, for my loose tongue and repeating lies that I've heard. I can see now that none of them are true. I have brought you a gift and hope you'll accept my apologies. Please, allow me to join in your Christmastide celebration." He turned to his squire. "Bryce, show the fair lady what I've brought her."

"Come on," growled the guard, taking Bryce by the arm. "You, too," he said to Adam.

"What a shame," said Adam with a forced sigh. "Bryce, I hope you're hungry since you and I will have to eat that entire goose by ourselves."

He took a step down one stair, hoping he had stirred the lady's interest. He had done his research before coming here. The word whispered through the rushes was that

Lady Eva Cavendish liked to eat. Hopefully, her hunger at the moment was stronger than her anger directed toward him.

"Wait!" she called out, causing Adam to stop in his tracks.

"Aye, my lady?" he asked, turning his head with a raised brow, sure his ploy had worked. "Was there something more?" He saw her eyes fastened to the covered platter in Bryce's hands. Then, when the tip of her pink tongue shot out to quickly lick her lips, he knew he'd be inside the castle within minutes.

"Let me see what you brought. Uncover the dish," she ordered, urgency sounding in her voice.

"Of course, my lady," Adam replied with a satisfied smile. "Bryce, remove the lid."

Carefully balancing the platter on one arm, Bryce reached out and picked up the lid with the other. The aroma of the garlic and rosemary roasted goose filled the air. Mingling together with that was the tantalizing scent of the quince, apple, and sage stuffing.

"My lady, I have bought and cooked the prized goose from the butcher's shop at the edge of town. I slowly turned and seared the fine meat on a spit over an outdoor fire for hours to give it a woodsy flavor. Then I gently stroked it with a golden liquid of exotic herbs infused with its own rich juices until the skin turned crispy. Afterwards, I gently laid it in a covered pot, coating it with a drizzling of sweet cider and red, robust wine, so it would stay succulent, juicy, and tender and not dry out."

Adam noticed her eyes grow wide as they fixated on the bird. As if in a trance, she blindly took a step closer. He had her right where he wanted her and so he continued.

"Just look at those plump quinces and golden apples that make up the stuffing." He reached out and moved Bryce's hand so the platter was closer to Eva. Then he held his fingers together and used them as a fan as he wafted at the air around the goose. "Can you smell the leeks and sage?" He made a big show of sniffing the air and releasing it with a sigh of satisfaction. "It smells so rich and nutty. And the velvety sauce made with the drippings has been topped off with just a sprinkle of cinnamon and mace. Did you want to sample it?"

"Aye," she said so eagerly that he half-expected to see saliva dribbling down her chin in anticipation. With one shaking hand, she greedily reached out for the goose.

"Allow me, my lady." Adam raised his hand to stop her. "The goose is hot and I wouldn't want you to burn your precious mouth." He used two fingers, grabbing a piece of meat folded over with a little stuffing in between. Holding it up, he blew on it to cool it off for her. Her mouth hung open as she watched his every move. Then he smiled and carefully held it up to her mouth.

Like a baby bird wanting to be fed, her jaw dropped open. Adam gently placed the meat in her mouth.

With an intake of breath and her eyes narrowing slightly, she chewed the goose slowly, savoring the flavor. "It's delicious," she said, her voice sounding almost orgasmic. "It's the best goose I've ever tasted in my life. I'd like more."

"Really?" Adam asked, brushing his hands together. "Well, I'm sorry, but my squire and I are going to eat the rest of the goose by ourselves as we celebrate Christmas in the cold out in our tent. Bryce, cover up the goose," he commanded with a flick of his wrist. "We want to save the heat that holds in all those tantalizing flavors." He nonchalantly looked over to the guard next. The man was also staring at the goose with want in his eyes. "All right, we are ready to go."

"Nay! Stay," Eva begged him as she hurriedly followed him down the stairs.

"What's that, my lady?" he asked, sarcastically holding a hand to his ear as he turned back to see the desperation in her eyes. There was no way she was going to let him leave now. Not after all that. Adam felt confident that it was one of his most persuasive performances to date.

"Why don't you and your squire bring the goose into the great hall," she suggested in a meek voice. The bold confidence he'd heard earlier in her words seemed to have suddenly disappeared. "You are welcome to join us for the meal."

Adam looked at her and cocked his head. "But, my lady, we are not on the guest list, or did you forget?"

She bit her lip and looked in the other direction. Her chest heaved in and out, giving notice to her full breasts hidden beneath the fabric. It was almost making him feel randy. He could tell she struggled with her decision as it took her a moment to answer. "I'll make sure your names get on the list," she finally said.

"Well, then, I guess we'll join you," said Adam with a wide smile. "My name, again, is Sir Adam de Ware, and my squire's name is Bryce." He bowed, just to be proper.

"Guard, let them pass," she commanded to her soldier. "They're with me."

"Aye, my lady," answered the guard, heading back down the stairs.

"This way, both of you," said Eva, motioning with her head toward the keep. "And whatever you do, don't drop the goose, you fools."

CHAPTER 2

KISSING BOUGHS AND THE LORD OF MISRULE

*L*ady Eva Cavendish entered the great hall with her guests trailing behind her. She was sure her father was going to like the Christmas goose brought by Sir Adam. This could be just what she needed to help her father regain his strength. She had never tasted anything so delicious in her life. It reminded her a lot of her late mother's cooking. But ever since her mother's death five years ago when Eva took over as Lady of the Castle, things had not been the same.

Eva couldn't get the cooks and servants to produce any food that, in her opinion, was worth eating. She had prayed for help not only with the food but also with her father's health. So when Sir Adam appeared on her doorstep on Christmas Eve, she realized he had to be a sign from God. Aye, perhaps this man was somehow an answer to her prayers. Things had to get better now.

"Sir Adam, you'll sit next to me at the dais. Your squire

11

will put the goose on the table and then eat below the salt with the others," she instructed.

"Of course, my lady," said the handsome Sir Adam, following her up the stairs to the raised platform where the nobility ate. The long table was covered with a white cloth and set for the holidays with plates and goblets made of silver. In front of the plates were candles in jars that were covered with holiday greenery. During the twelve days of Christmas, the nobles made sure that everything was at its best.

The man had dark brown hair and a small mustache and beard. His amazing, bright blue eyes scanned the room, taking in his surroundings like a bird of prey. This knight was alert and aware but, at the same time, his blue orbs seemed to hold many secrets behind them. His brows were thick and craggy. A padded gambeson covered his chest and leather wrist guards and a mail hauberk marked him as a seasoned warrior. For such a cold night, she found it surprising that he didn't even wear a cape.

"Father, this is Sir Adam de Ware," she said when they reached the center seat of the dais. "Sir Adam, this is Earl Albert Cavendish. And next to him is my grandmother, Lady Barbara."

"My lady," said Adam, taking her grandmother's hand and kissing it. He bowed at the waist and held one hand behind his back. His half-closed eyes glanced down at her grandmother's hand and then up to settle on her eyes. Lady Barbara blushed and smiled. He had good manners and was quite charming, even with older women it seemed.

"Nice to meet you, Sir Adam," said her grandmother, loving the attention.

Next, Adam turned to the earl and bowed again. "Thank you for your hospitality on this cold night, Earl," said Adam, reaching out to shake her father's hand.

Her father turned his head and grunted. "Aye," he mumbled, but said nothing more. Adam moved his hand closer, still waiting for the earl to shake it. Eva held her breath. Her father wouldn't respond in the expected way because he couldn't.

"That's enough!" snapped Eva, not wanting Adam to know of her father's condition. It was better if he thought the man was just being rude. "Take your seat. The meal will start now."

Eva didn't want to sound like a shrew, but she had to say something to stop Adam from asking questions. Since her father's fall from his horse six months ago, he no longer had control over the right side of his body. This was her family's secret and Eva would do anything to keep it from others. She especially didn't want the king to know her father was no longer capable of serving him. Never again would the earl be able to fight for King Edward, let alone rule his own castle. A secret like this being revealed could ruin her father as well as her family name.

It was no secret that Eva was thought of by everyone as cruel and cold-hearted, but she no longer cared. Ever since the death of her mother, she had closed herself off to others and kept her feelings and thoughts locked away deep inside her. It was easier that way. Eva didn't deal well with death. Her siblings having died through the years only hampered instead of helped her overcome her fear of losing those she loved. She had to be strong, she told herself, never showing how vulnerable she really was in this kind of situation. Aye, she had to be there to support her family, and she would be until the day she died. Eva didn't want to lose her father because he meant the world to her.

Eva also didn't want Cavendish Castle to be taken from her family. This was her home and had been for her entire life. There were many memories, both good and bad, within these stone walls. To think of possibly losing it all scared her out of her mind.

Only the healer and her grandmother knew her father's awful secret. Together, they devised the story that his leg was temporarily broken and the healer had put a splint on it. Actually, it had been broken, but was healed months ago. Prolonging it was really a ploy because her father could no longer walk. The blacksmith added wheels to the earl's chair so they could push him around.

Aye, Eva had done whatever she could to keep quiet the fact that her father was no longer an able-bodied man. The earl would never again be able to use his sword arm according to the healer. Lately, his speech had become quite slurred, and he sometimes acted worse than the court fool. Eva normally told everyone he was well in his cups trying to combat the pain from his leg that refused to heal. But after six months now, people were starting to ask questions. These were questions she would never be able to answer without revealing the truth.

"Sir Adam," she said, cutting off pieces of the goose and laying them on her father's trencher. "Tell me, how is it that a knight knows how to cook?"

ADAM WATCHED the woman hack away at the goose, her actions about causing him to cry out. She didn't know how to handle a knife, nor did she respect the bird that was to be their meal. "Allow me, my lady," he said, taking the knife and serving spoon from her and cutting the meat in a proper way.

"Thank you, Sir Knight," she said, through her teeth. "However, I am capable of doing that myself." She tried to grab the knife back from him, but he stood up and pulled the platter toward him.

"I'm surprised you don't have your servants do this." Adam looked up to see her grandmother handing a goblet of wine to her father. The earl took it with his left hand. Something was odd about the man but he couldn't quite put his finger on it yet.

"You were going to tell me how you know how to cook such a delectable, tasty goose," Eva said, taking his attention, even though he'd yet to say a word about it.

"Well, if you must know, I learned as a child." He placed some food on her plate and she eagerly dove in to eat it. "I grew up being raised by a nursemaid since my mother was sickly and died shortly after I was born."

"Aye, my mother died, too, five years ago," she said, turning the conversation to her even though she had asked about him.

"I am sorry to hear that." Adam cut another piece of meat and held it out to the earl. "May I have your plate, Earl?" he asked. The man looked over at him and scowled.

"Here you are." Eva quickly picked up her father's plate and held it out to Adam. After she put it down in front of the man, she picked up an eating spoon and handed it to her father. Once again, the man took it with his left hand.

"Oh, I see your father is left-handed," said Adam, placing food on his own plate.

"Nay, he's not," she said taking another bite of goose. Then her eyes opened wide and she glanced at the earl and then him. She cleared her throat and put down her spoon. "I mean, my father thinks it's important to be able to use both hands just as accurately so he purposely uses his left hand to make it stronger."

"I see." Adam sat back down to eat his food. "Getting back to my story, I spent a lot of time in the kitchen. You see, the nursemaid was having an affair with the stable-master and left me with the cooks most of the time. I didn't mind because I liked to eat . . . just like you do."

She stopped chewing and released her spoon. Folding her hands on her lap, she threw him an icy stare. "I don't eat any more or less than any other lady. What is it you are trying to say, Sir Adam?"

"I only meant that I am pleased the goose is to your liking. I heard that you were looking for a good cook and

16

that is why I brought it." He'd heard no such thing but thought he'd take the chance that it might be true. He needed a reason to stay here and, hopefully, this would work to his advantage.

"Aye. I am looking for a good cook," she admitted. "Ever since my mother died, the staff seems to be serving tasteless and often rancid food. If my father's leg is going to heal, he needs nourishment and food that is tasty and properly cooked."

"What happened to him?" asked Adam, scooping up some stewed root vegetables and taking a bite. He almost gagged. The food was horrible, she wasn't jesting. He quickly washed it down with a swig of ale.

"My father broke his leg when he was thrown from a horse. He'll be better soon and will be up and walking again, so there is no need to worry."

Adam eyed the man's leg under the table that stuck out straight and was wrapped in a splint. He also noticed wheels on the chair. "I wasn't worried, but it seems as if you are." He watched for her reaction. Her jaw became tight and she sat up straight. "How long has his leg been in a splint?"

"It doesn't matter," she retorted.

A messenger boy ran up with a missive in his hand and bowed. "Good earl, a messenger of the king is here to see you."

"What do mean?" Eva's head snapped up.

"Here he comes now," said Adam, spying the messenger of the king walk in and stop at the foot of the table.

"Earl Cavendish, the king has sent this message." He held out the missive with two hands but the earl did nothing to take it.

"His leg is broken and he can't reach that far, you fool," snapped Eva, reaching across the table. "Give it to me."

"Nay, allow me," said Adam, jumping up and reaching over her to snatch the missive from the boy.

"Sir Adam! What are you doing here?" asked the boy, recognizing him from usually being at the king's side.

"Shhh," said Adam, shaking his head to tell the boy to remain quiet. "Thank you, you are dismissed," he said, sending the boy away.

"Give me that." Eva's hand shot out. But before she could get the missive, Adam reached over her and handed it to the earl. "Here you go, Earl."

The man looked up but didn't take it. "I'm eating now," he grumbled.

"My father's hands are greasy. I'll read it for him." Eva tried once again to get the parchment from him but Adam quickly opened it instead.

"Allow me to read it for you, Earl Cavendish." He managed to scan the contents of the missive before Eva pulled it out of his hand.

"How dare you suppose you have the right to read a missive that was sent to my father from the king."

"What does it say?" asked the earl, not turning his head at all when he spoke.

Eva scanned the contents and shoved the missive into a

pouch hanging from her side. "We'll talk about it later, Father."

Adam wanted to say something, but decided to remain quiet. After the meal, the servants began to clear away the tables for dancing while the musicians tuned up their lutes, harps and even a hurdy-gurdy.

"Here ye, here ye," called out the herald getting everyone's attention. "Now, Jameson, who has been named the Lord of Misrule, will take over with running the Christmas festivities." A young boy of about four and ten years of age stepped forward and bowed to the crowd.

"Lord of Misrule?" Adam chuckled. "It seems as if you'll have a wild celebration on your hands now, my lady." Adam was familiar with the tradition. By chance, the Lord of Misrule was chosen by who found a bean hidden in their cake. His title during the holidays made him not only in charge of the games but also able to rule during the Christmastide festivities. He could make anyone do anything he wanted. Therefore, a peasant could be ordered to act like a noble and a noble might end up in the scullery for the night. But most of the directions from the Lord of Misrule had to do with drinking games.

"Jameson is the son of one our knights and also a page," Eva told him. "He was chosen by luck of the draw, but I am sure he can be trusted. I specifically warned him not to do anything that would cause embarrassment to any of the nobles."

"But that's not the way it works," protested Adam. "It seems to me, you have taken away control from the Lord of Misrule as well as from your father in ruling his castle. Why is that, my lady?"

Eva scowled and threw her nose in the air. "You know nothing, Sir Adam, and I don't like your attitude. I will allow you to stay the night in the castle since you brought me the goose. However, in the morning, you and your squire will leave anon."

"I see," he said, eying the Lord of Misrule who was laughing and ordering some of the men to chug down ale while dancing with the women. "I apologize if I insulted you. May I beg your forgiveness and ask for one dance tonight before I see to the road in the morning?"

She hesitated a minute as if she were giving it some thought. Her eyes settled on the goose and she made her decision. "I suppose one dance is all right, but no more."

"Of course, my lady, just one," he answered with a bow.

"Let me tend to my father first and I'll be right with you."

Adam hurried over to talk to his squire before Eva returned. "Bryce," he said, calling him over.

"Aye, my lord?" asked Bryce, chewing on a sweet meat as he joined him.

"Lady Eva is sending us away in the morning and I can't have that. So I have something I need you to do." He dug into his pocket and pulled out a gold crown. "Here, give this to the Lord of Misrule," he instructed.

"What for?" Bryce held up the coin to survey it. "This is quite a sum."

"Give him the message that I want him to send me to work in the kitchen as a cook through Twelfth Night."

"Twelfth Night? But that means you'd be a cook for the entire twelve days of Christmas." Bryce laughed heartily. "You must be jesting."

"Nay, I mean it. I need a reason to stay here so I can complete my mission. Since the Lord of Misrule can order anyone to do anything during his reign, this is perfect. Lady Eva won't be able to send me away after all."

"Makes sense. All right, I'll do it." Bryce flipped the coin in the air and Adam snatched it away.

"Don't do that." Adam scanned the room, hoping no one saw his squire flipping the gold coin. "Tell the Lord of Misrule that this money is also to keep him quiet. He is to tell no one that I requested him to make me a cook. Do you understand? I don't want Lady Eva to know."

"I understand, my lord. I'll go right away."

"Good." Adam slapped the coin back into the squire's hand just as Eva headed in his direction. "One more thing," he told Bryce in a low voice.

"What is it, my lord?"

"Get the Lord of Misrule to also order Lady Eva to kiss me under the mistletoe."

Bryce chuckled. "She won't like that."

"She won't like the idea, but I assure you she is going to love being kissed by me. Now hurry, here she comes."

"As you say." Bryce left just as Lady Eva approached.

"My father will need me in his solar, so let's make this a quick dance," she told him.

"My lady." Adam bowed and held out his arm as the music started. Gently laying her hand atop his arm, they proceeded to dance.

"Do tell me more about your father," said Adam, trying to gain information as well as to break the silence between them.

"I don't care to talk about my father and I would appreciate it if you stopped asking me questions." The song ended and she pulled away. "You and your squire can sleep in the great hall tonight but come first light, I want both of you gone."

Adam was about to say something else to keep her from leaving when the Lord of Misrule jumped atop a bench and held up his hand.

"Here ye, here ye, the Lord of Misrule speaks," called out the boy.

"Good night, Sir Adam." Lady Eva turned to go. But when she heard the Lord of Misrule's announcement, she stopped dead in her tracks.

"I command Lady Eva to kiss the visiting Sir Adam de Ware under the mistletoe," said the boy.

LADY EVA SPUN around in surprise to find the crowd watching her, smiling and laughing. The fool, Sir Adam, stepped under one of the kissing boughs and looked at her, shrugging his shoulders.

"Nay," she said, shaking her head. She couldn't kiss a stranger, especially in front of everyone.

"My lady, the Lord of Misrule has given us a command," Sir Adam told her. "Isn't it true that during these twelve days of Christmas, the Lord of Misrule can order nobles as well as peasants to do what he wants and no one can object?"

"Well, yes, but this is different," she answered.

"How so?" yelled someone from the crowd.

"I'm Lady of the Castle," she said, feeling very uncomfortable.

"I'm a noble, too," a knight called out. "And yet the Lord of Misrule has commanded me to give up my seat at the dais to a servant."

"I was told to clean out the stable," said someone else.

"If you don't kiss Sir Adam, then we shouldn't have to do what the Lord of Misrule tells us either," came the voice of a brave woman from the crowd.

Lady Eva didn't want trouble. Everyone knew that during these twelve days of Christmas, the Lord of Misrule was in charge. If she backed out, so would everyone else. Then there would be trouble and her father would be summoned to handle it all. She didn't want her father in that position. He couldn't hold his court in his condition because, if so, he would be exposed. She had no choice other than to kiss the knight after all.

"Fine," she spat, picking up the hem of her gown and trudging through the rushes to make her way to the man. She stopped in front of him and looked up. The kissing bough hung directly over Sir Adam's head.

It was a custom for men and women to steal kisses

from each other under the bough during the Christmas season. There were at least a dozen of these orbs hanging from the rafters. The kissing boughs were constructed from metal frames bent into the shapes of globes. Attached to each was greenery that included pine boughs, holly, and mistletoe. If it hadn't been unlucky to bring ivy inside, that winter greenery would have been added as well. Apples were hung from the bottoms of the pieces. Around the tops of the spheres were lit beeswax candles. The structures were actually quite large.

"Come, my lady. Everyone is watching." Sir Adam waited for her with outstretched arms. Eva wanted to slap the smile right off his face. The sooner she kissed him the sooner she could retire for the evening. And in the morning, Sir Adam would be gone.

She took a step closer and puckered her lips, closing her eyes, dreading the action.

"Not like that," she heard him say with a chuckle. "Like this."

Before she knew what was happening, Sir Adam pulled her up close to his body and wrapped his arms around her tightly. Her eyes popped open to see him lowering his face to hers. She didn't even have a chance to say a word. His mouth covered hers and he kissed her passionately like a lover.

The sounds of the crowd oohing and aahing were drowned out by the rapid drumming of her heart in her ears. She actually enjoyed the kiss, although she never expected she would. His lips were sensual but strong and his kiss was caressing instead of forceful. Her eyes closed as her head tilted back when he pulled away. And then to her surprise, he kissed her again and she did nothing to stop it. Eva got lost in the fantasy of being in the arms of an honorable knight while being treated like a lover at the same time. It was a memorable experience that she would never forget. It took her a moment to remember everyone was watching them.

"That's enough," she said, pushing away from him and straightening her gown, not able to meet his eyes after what had just happened between them.

"My lady, you seemed as if you enjoyed the kiss but yet you are acting appalled. It is not as if the Lord of Misrule ordered you to clean out the gong pit. It was naught but a harmless kiss." Adam chuckled softly.

"Sir Adam, since this is the last time I'll be seeing you in my castle, I choose not to respond to that." Eva turned to leave but, once again, was stopped by the Lord of Misrule's words.

"Sir Adam de Ware," said the man in charge of the festivities. "I have made another decision concerning you."

"You have?" asked Adam. "And what might that be?"

"You are to be sent to the kitchen to cook from now until Twelfth Night."

The crowd laughed heartily at this announcement. Never would a knight be caught in the kitchen doing the job of a servant. Only by the command of the Lord of Misrule during the Christmastide season would this ever happen. Lady Eva turned around slowly, unable to believe what she'd just heard. She'd warned the boy not to embarrass any of the nobles and yet he continued to do so and she could do nothing about it.

"It seems I'll be staying around for a while yet, my lady," said Sir Adam, grinning from ear to ear. "Do let me know what you'd like to eat throughout the rest of the Christmas festivities."

Eva turned on her heel and stormed out of the room, holding back her scream of frustration. Sir Adam de Ware was proving to be a thorn in her side, and she was going to have to remedy this soon.

CHAPTER 3

CHURCH BELLS

*E*va paced back and forth in her father's solar, regretting that she had ever allowed Sir Adam into her keep.

"Bid the devil, Daughter. Stop your infernal pacing," complained her father from his bed. "It is driving me mad."

"We need to do something about this," said Eva, looking over to her grandmother sitting in a chair doing needlework. The healer, an older man, leaned over the bed checking her father's condition by pricking him with the tip of a knife on his bad arm and leg.

"Stop pricking my skin," growled the earl, speaking in a slurred voice since the right side of his mouth drooped when he spoke. "How many times do I have to tell you I can't feel a bloody thing?"

"I'm sorry, my lord." The healer placed the knife in his bag and backed away from the bed.

"My dear, you are overreacting a bit," said her grandmother, Lady Barbara, concentrating on her needlework as she spoke. "Sir Adam is very charming. You seemed to enjoy his kiss. So what difference does it make if he stays or goes?"

"Healer, leave us," commanded Eva with a wave of dismissal. "Come back first thing in the morning. Remember not to say a word about the earl's condition or about anything we've talked about behind closed doors." She handed the man a coin from her pouch to keep him silent.

"Aye, my lady," said the man, bowing and taking the coin with two hands. Once he left the room and closed the door, Eva continued.

"Sir Adam can't stay. He is already asking too many questions," Eva explained.

"The man sure knows how to cook a goose. I'd like to see what else he can cook," said Lord Albert.

"Father, he's a knight. He has no business being in the kitchen." This aggravated Eva to no end. "I told the Lord of Misrule not to choose any of the nobles when he handed out his ridiculous tasks. I swear I'll have the boy flogged for this when it is all over."

"Calm down, Eva," said her grandmother. "You know as well as us that the cooks cannot make a dish worth eating. Mayhap, Sir Adam will be an asset in the kitchen. He didn't seem to mind being put there."

"Nay, he didn't." This made Eva suspicious. Most knights would fight it tooth and nail rather than to be caught doing the work of a servant, especially cooking.

Adam, on the other hand, just stood there and grinned. "I must admit, I do like the fact that we'll have some tasty food for a change. But the missive from the king worries me." She pulled the missive out of her pouch to read it again.

"What's that, my dear?" asked the earl, his eyes closing as he began to drift off to sleep. With his condition, the man tired easily. Eva wanted him to rest and didn't want to upset him.

"It's nothing, Father. I will handle everything." She walked over and gave him a kiss on the head as he drifted off to sleep.

"It's nothing?" asked Lady Barbara. "We both know a missive from the king cannot be good." Her eyes flashed upward to scrutinize Eva. "What does the missive say?"

Eva sighed and slipped the parchment back into her pouch. "It's from King Edward, Grandmother. I think he is getting suspicious from all the missives from father declining to meet with him. It's been too long and I can't keep using the excuse that he cannot fight because of his leg. Now, the king is coming here himself on Twelfth Night for a visit and to talk with Father."

"Nay, he can't." Her grandmother shoved the needle-work back into the basket and got to her feet. "We don't want the king here. You'll have to write another missive and send it immediately to keep him away. If he comes to Cavendish, there is no doubt that he'll learn the truth."

"And if he does, we will lose everything." Eva sadly looked back at her father sleeping on the bed. He had no idea she'd been forging his signature after writing missives to the king for the past six months. She'd even used her father's signet ring to seal the missive by stamping his crest into the hot wax.

"You're going to have to move quickly," warned Lady Barbara. "Twelfth Night will be here soon."

"I will, Grandmother." Suddenly feeling deflated, Eva had no idea what to do. "I'm afraid I will not be able to keep up this charade for long. If Sir Adam discovers what we've been trying to hide, he's likely to tell the bishop who will in turn tell the king. We all might be locked in the dungeon, and Father might even be killed for my deception." Eva felt like crying. The stress of this all was getting hard to bear.

"Eva, I know your father too well since he is my son." The old woman put her arm around Eva's shoulders. "Albert would not want to live if his title, castle, lands, and all his securities were taken from him. I'm surprised that, in his condition, he hasn't tried to take his own life by now."

"Nay, don't say that!" Eva clung to her grandmother. Her father snored loudly on the bed in the midst of a deep sleep. "Father would never do that."

"He is a proud man, Eva. When your mother died, as well as your siblings through the years, a small part of him died along with them. I no longer see the same life in his eyes that used to be there. He hardly ever smiles."

"Aye, he used to laugh but is never happy anymore," Eva

agreed. "He does seem to be slipping away from us quickly. How long did the healer say he has to live?"

"No one knows for sure," answered her grandmother.

"Grandmother, sometimes I wonder if we should have told the king the truth as soon as Father had his accident. But now, it's too late. We can't divulge the secret or we will all be sentenced. I wish this had never happened."

"Nay, you did the right thing," said the old woman. "No one can know the truth."

"Perhaps you're right," answered Eva with a deep sigh. "I guess we can only hope that by some miracle Father will recover. If so, the king will never need to know that we deceived him, even if it was for the benefit of Father."

The bells of St. Mary's Church in the village rang out loud and clear, announcing it was midnight and time for the Christmas mass to begin. At the same time, someone knocked at the door.

Eva walked over to open it, surprised to see Sir Adam standing there.

"What do you want?" she snapped.

"My lady, it is already midnight and the mass has begun. I've come to escort you, if you please."

"Nay, I don't please. Now leave me alone." She tried to close the door but his hand gripped it and stopped it from closing.

"I am sure you will be attending mass as is proper for a woman of your position." It was more of a command than a question. It should have upset her, but she knew he was right. It was Christmas. There were only midnight masses twice a year, on Christmas Eve and Easter. It would be a sin to miss this special service on such a holy day.

"All right, let's go." As she pushed the door open, Adam looked inside.

"What about your grandmother and father? I'll escort them as well."

"Nay! Nay," she said. "Father's leg is acting up and he is already sleeping."

"Then I'll escort you, Lady Barbara." Adam held out his arm and nodded to the old woman.

"I'll be going to mass in the morning with my son," announced Lady Barbara. "I'll stay and watch over him tonight. You two go on without me."

Eva tried to give her grandmother a signal not to leave her alone with Sir Adam. But her grandmother smiled knowingly, and walked over and closed the door behind them.

* * *

LATER THAT NIGHT after midnight mass, Adam entered the solar that he'd been assigned to use for the duration of his stay. His squire was already there waiting.

"What did she say, my lord?" Bryce asked curiously. "Did you find out any information why the earl has been avoiding the king?"

"Nay, I learned absolutely nothing." Adam unclasped his weapon belt and hung it on a hook on the wall. Then he started to undress as he spoke. "I thought by escorting

Lady Eva and her family to church, I'd learn more. But her grandmother and the earl didn't go. And Lady Eva didn't say two words to me the entire time. I'm afraid I'm going to have to find another way to draw her family secrets out of her."

"How?" asked Bryce. "She doesn't seem willing to tell you anything nor does she even seem to like you."

"Mayhap not, but I am going to change all that starting tomorrow." Adam collapsed atop the bed and put his arms behind his head.

"How so, my lord? Are you going to come out and ask her point blank what is going on here?"

"Nay. That'll never work. However, I have another way in mind that will turn Lady Eva to clay in my hands just waiting to be formed."

"Do tell me," said the squire anxiously.

"I'm going to seduce her . . . with food."

"With food?" Bryce looked confused.

"I have been assigned to her kitchen until Twelfth Night and I am going to use it to my advantage. You noticed that Lady Eva likes to eat, didn't you?"

"Well, I suppose she does seem to require food of good taste and she certainly looks as if she enjoys it."

"Then that is what I'm going to give her. Good food that she will enjoy. Each day from now until Twelfth Night, I will make exquisite dishes that will tantalize her taste buds and cause her to beg for more."

"Can you do that, my lord?"

"Do you even doubt me? After all, I am probably the

only knight alive who can whip up a dish that is fit for a king. And I will use my skill to seduce Lady Eva's secrets right out from under her. Before long, she'll no longer despise me but, instead, she'll desire me, even if it is only for my food."

Adam chuckled and closed his eyes. And behind those closed lids, all he could see was Lady Eva in his arms as they shared a kiss under the kissing bough. After all, he had enjoyed it just as much as she.

CHAPTER 4

PARTRIDGE WITH PEARS AND UMBLE PIE

"*I*'ll require to see your undercroft as well as your larder," Adam told Eva the next day as they entered the kitchen together.

"Sir Adam, it is inappropriate of you to ask a lady such a thing," Eva answered with a sniff. "I'll summon my steward to show you what you need to see."

"My lady, if I am to cook the meals from now until Twelfth Night to your liking for the Christmastide celebration, I'll need you to tell me what you desire."

"What I desire?" For some reason, these words made Eva look at him and blush. She lowered her head and glanced up at him shyly. "No one has ever asked me before what I desired. I must admit, Sir Adam, that I have no skill in cooking and neither do I pretend to be an expert where food is concerned. But I will tell you that some of the dishes my late mother used to make I truly enjoyed. None of the cooks have been able to duplicate her recipes, and even the servants who knew how to construct them can't seem to do it properly anymore."

"What's in your larder?"

"It is stocked full for the Christmas season since my father's men have recently returned from a hunt."

"Did your father go with them?" he asked, hoping to learn as much information as possible.

"Of course not. Didn't you see his leg in a splint?"

"How long did you say it has been that way?"

"I have much to do, Sir Adam, and cannot indulge in the art of small talk. Now, if you want me to show you the larder, we will go now."

"All right. We'll go then." Adam held out his arm to escort her. She looked at his arm and then up to his face. She seemed hesitant but gently placed her hand on his arm. He took his free arm and covered her hand with his fingers as they walked. Her skin was warm and soft and the scent of rosewater wafted up from her body making him slightly heady. Lady Eva was a beautiful woman and it was only her demeanor that probably scared off any suitor.

They entered the cool cellar room where the meat was stored. Adam lit a candle. His eyes opened wide when he saw the amount of salted meat hanging from hooks.

"I didn't expect this," he said, wandering over to inspect a hanging sow and then a carcass of a deer. "And what is in all these barrels?" He splayed out his arm, motioning to the dozens of barrels lining the floor.

"Most of them have meat that has been put down in lard to store it. Others have salted herring and fish."

"Nay, no fish," he said, waving his hand through the air.

"I enjoy fish," she told him.

"Since everyone has had to abstain from meat during Advent, fish would not be an appropriate Christmas meal."

"Whatever you think," she said in a small voice.

"What is stored in your undercroft?" asked Adam.

"There are a lot of barrels, but I honestly don't know what's in them," she explained. "Since my mother's passing, the cooks seldom go down in the undercroft because they don't like it there. They use other items instead."

"Don't go down in the undercroft?" he asked, appalled. "And you don't order them to do it?"

"I have been very busy assisting my father, so I didn't see what difference it made where they got their ingredients. As long as there is food on the table, that is all that matters."

"Is it?" he asked, making a tsking sound with his tongue. "If you don't mind my saying so, my lady, it seems to me this castle is in need of a leader."

"I do mind you saying so, and I won't have you speaking like that again," she snapped. "I am wasting time with you. Use whatever you like and if you need something else, send one of my servants down to the docks to buy it from the tradesmen. My steward will give you whatever money you need. Now, get to work because I'll expect these meals to be as good as the goose."

"They'll be better," he said with a promise. Then he reached out and caressed her cheek with his hand, watching as her face softened and her eyes closed slightly.

The firelight danced on her skin giving it a seductive glow. He couldn't help himself. He leaned over and kissed her on the lips, longing to taste her once again. He was expecting a reaction similar to the one when he kissed her under the kissing bough. Instead, she pulled away and slapped him. "What was that for?" he asked.

"That was to remind you of your position."

"I am a nobleman," he said proudly.

"Aye, but you are also a cook for the next twelve days, so don't forget it." She stormed out of the larder, leaving him standing there alone in the cool, dank room. Lady Eva Cavendish was going to be more of a challenge to seduce than he originally thought.

Walking over to survey the contents of the larder, he spotted exactly what he needed swinging by a rope from the rafters. He walked up to it and looked upward, smiling. If this didn't soften her hard composure, nothing would. He had his work cut out for him and he wasn't going to let her treat him this way again. Before long, she would be coming to him begging for more. If he gave it to her or not depended on what she could do for him.

Pulling his dagger from his waist belt, he reached up and cut down the partridge, knowing just how to prepare it to make her mouth water.

* * *

"EVA, WHERE HAVE YOU BEEN?" asked Lady Barbara when Eva finally returned to her father's solar. The healer was there, tending to her father. "I thought you were going to be here an hour ago."

"I'm sorry, Grandmother. I got caught up with some details and I apologize that I'm late."

"Your father has taken a turn for the worse."

"Nay!" She rushed over to the bed and grabbed her father's hand in hers. "What's happened?" she asked the healer.

"Lord Albert has taken ill with a fever. He is talking nonsense and hasn't opened his eyes but a few times all morning," said the healer. "I'm going to use leeches to suck out any infection." The man took a jar out of his bag and held it up. Inside were blood-sucking leeches stuck to the inside of the jar.

"I cannot stay here and watch this." Holding a hand to her stomach, Eva headed back to the door.

"Eva, wait!" Lady Barbara used her cane as she hobbled across the floor. "What about the missive?" she whispered, looking over her shoulder to see if the healer had heard her.

"I'll write it later," she said, feeling her stomach rumble. "I have to meet with the reeve since it is Quarter Day. All the rents are due and need to be collected from the tenants. I also need to oversee the decorating of the great hall for the Christmastide festivities. After that, I'll go to mass and then join you at the Christmas feast. I hope Father will be able to sit at the dais today."

"He's ill and shouldn't be moved," said the healer.

"You went to mass last night," her grandmother reminded her. "Surely, you don't need to go again today."

"It is Christmas Day," snapped Eva, feeling the stress of the situation upon her. "Father needs to be sitting at the dais or there are going to be wagging tongues plus more questions from Sir Adam that I don't want to answer. Healer, do what you have to do in order to make him well enough to participate at the meal today."

"Aye, my lady," said the healer, placing the leeches onto her father's arms and legs.

Feeling sick, Eva turned and started out the door.

"You never told me why you are going to mass again," said her grandmother.

"I feel the need," Eva answered, thinking about the improper dream she had about coupling with Sir Adam last night. When he kissed her again today in the larder, she had to slap him. If not, she would have been lifting her skirts herself to live out the dream. Aye, she needed to go to mass again as well as confession. And most of all, she needed to stay far away from Sir Adam de Ware.

* * *

"Take the Boar's Head and Brawn up to the dais," Adam instructed the servants later that day. "Make sure the courses follow quickly as Lady Eva likes to eat and I don't want her to have to wait for the food."

"Aye, my lord," answered one of the servants.

Adam picked up the platter containing his secret

weapon and headed directly over to Lady Eva who was at the dais, leaning over and talking to her father. Her grandmother was at the earl's other side and looked upset about something.

The herald blared out a few notes on his straight trumpet and the musicians joined in with a royal tune. The Christmas procession of food was brought into the room. Adam looked down to the roasted partridge with pears and smiled. He had outdone himself once again. Even he was salivating at the wonderful aromas. Picking up the platter, he brought his offering into the great hall.

"MY LADY."

Eva looked up to see Adam approaching the dais with a covered platter in his hands. She quickly placed the goblet in her father's left hand and turned around to face Adam.

"Sir Adam. What have you got there?"

"I'm sure you've already seen the Christmas Boar's Head and Brawn." He nodded toward the platter with the boar's head that graced the table. It had a baked apple in its mouth and cloves made up its eyes.

"Aye, you did a wonderful job. The Christmas Boar looks and smells delicious."

"I've also made venison in a rich sauce, rabbit stew, and a variety of braised vegetables. But my biggest surprise for you is this." He laid the platter down right in front of Eva and opened the lid. Surprised gasps went up from the table.

"Sir Adam, what is it?" she asked, eying up the monstrosity.

"It is partridge with pears in a robust wine sauce infused with plump mulberries and spicy ginger, my lady. I have roasted the partridge on a spit, rubbing it gently in its own juices mixed with a variety of herbs. Then, for the occasion, I dressed up the partridge to look like a knight."

"Aye, you have," she said with a giggle. The partridge sat upright on the platter with a small gourd stuck into the opening neck cavity to make a head. Cloves were its eyes and a slice of apple made up its beak. The bird was dressed in cloth clothes that were sewn to look like that of a knight. The partridge even held an eating knife in its wing. "It is beautiful as well as very creative, Sir Adam. Thank you."

"Don't thank me until you have tasted the finished product, my lady." He proceeded to cut off a piece and place it on her trencher. Today, instead of the silver plates, trenchers of stale bread were being used to hold their food. After the meal, the trenchers would be given as alms to the poor.

"Mmmmm. It's good," she said, savoring a piece in her mouth, almost screaming out because it was so delectable.

"How about a little warm mead to go with it?" Adam flagged down the ewerer who poured her some of the hot, fermented honey drink infused with spices.

Eva was in heaven. She hadn't tasted food this good

since her mother was alive. Lost in the experience, she didn't even realize that Adam was handing her father a trencher of meat. Since her father's goblet was in his left hand, Adam handed the food to his right hand, waiting for him to take it.

"Here you are, Good Earl," said Adam, still waiting. "Did you need a bigger cut of the meat?"

"Nay, I'm good and that is good and everything is good," mumbled the earl, dazed and flushed in the face.

"What did you say?" Adam looked confused and leaned closer to try to decipher the earl's words.

"He said thank you, it looks good," Eva blurted out. "Oh, who is that?" she asked, pointing in the opposite direction so Adam had to turn his head to look. In the meantime, she took the trencher from him and lifted her father's right hand, placing it atop it.

"Do you mean my squire?" Adam turned back, his eyes shooting down to the earl's trencher and then back up to her.

"I suppose it is your squire. I didn't recognize him." Eva picked up a serving spoon and ladled some of the pears along with the sauce over her partridge. "Thank you, Sir Adam. You may go back to the kitchen now." The sooner she dismissed him, the better. She didn't want him too close to her father because he was a very observant man.

Eva had just finished eating and spoke to the healer and her grandmother to take her father back to his solar when Bryce passed by with a good dozen palm-sized pies on a tray. She noticed he walked out the door into the courtyard. Curious as to what he was doing, she followed.

"Squire," she called out, running after him into the cold. She'd left so quickly she hadn't even had the chance to don her cloak.

"Aye, my lady?" Bryce turned around with a questioning look upon his brow.

"What is that and where are you going with it?" she snapped. "All food is to be kept in the great hall."

"Aye, my lady. However, Sir Adam sent me back to the kitchen to get more umble pies to give to the poor."

"He did, did he? And where is Sir Adam right now?"

"He's at the castle gate giving out trenchers as well as cooked geese and umble pies to those in need."

This infuriated Eva and she wasn't going to stand for it. "Give me that tray," she said, all but snatching it from the squire's hand. She stormed up to the front gate. "Sir Adam," she called out. "What is the meaning of this?"

Adam handed a few trenchers and also a cooked goose to a woman with three small children.

"Eat it in good health," he told the woman, giving one of her children a pat on the head. He turned to Eva and looked down to the tray of umble pies from her. Umble pies were made from the inners left over after cooking a deer. They were usually given to the poor. "Oh, wait," he called out to the woman. "Here is an umble pie for each of your children." He proceeded to take the pies off the tray and hand them to the children. "Be careful. They're hot and I don't want you to burn yourself."

"Thank you, my lord," said the woman, trying to curtsey while holding on to the food as well as the hand of her youngest son. "I am a widow and have no coin to buy food to feed my children. We would have gone hungry tonight if it wasn't for you."

"Don't thank me," said Adam. "It was Lady Eva's wish that you have it."

"Lady Eva, you are an angel and I cannot tell you how much this means to me." The woman curtseyed and thanked her a few more times before turning and leaving with her children. Now, Eva didn't feel as if she could be so harsh with Adam. Why did the woman have to thank her? After hearing that she was a widow and her children would have gone hungry on Christmas, Eva couldn't bring herself to reprimand Adam after all. No child or woman should go hungry, especially on a holiday.

"Sir Adam, I don't mind you giving out the umble pies and trenchers, but I hope you have at least been charging these people for the geese you've been handing out from my larder."

"Charging? Whatever for?" asked Adam.

"You do realize that the church has a fixed price of seven pence for a cooked goose and six pence for an uncooked bird."

"That is the church, not us," he said, taking a few more umble pies and handing them out to the beggars, smiling and wishing them all a good night. "Most of these people don't even make six pence for an entire week's wages let alone a day's. Plus, they had to pay you rent today, on

Christmas. Without any money left, most of them would have gone hungry. I'm sure you don't want that, do you, my lady? Didn't you hear that woman call you an angel?"

Eva did hear it and it only put her in an awkward position. No one had ever called her an angel before. It felt good. It felt right.

"Here," she said, shoving the empty tray into Adam's hands. She shivered and wrapped her arms around her. Adam was wearing a cloak and looked warm.

"Squire, take this," said Adam, handing Bryce the tray. Then he proceeded to remove his cloak and wrap it around her shoulders.

"What are you doing?" she asked.

"I see you shivering and your teeth chattering," he remarked. "Take my cloak, as I have already warmed it."

It did feel warm from his body heat, and the thought of being wrapped in his clothes seemed very intimate. It smelled like roasted goose from the kitchen and held a pine scent from Adam who seemed to spend a lot of time outdoors.

Music floated by on the breeze as carolers sang Christmas songs in front of a manger and danced in a circle in the courtyard.

"May I escort you over to the Christmas crib?" asked Adam, holding out his arm. "The Christmas play should be starting shortly."

"But you're not dressed for this weather," she protested. "You'll freeze without your cloak."

"Then we'll share it," he said, slipping his arm around

46

her waist before she knew what was happening. "Our bodies pushed close together beneath this cloak will enable us to share the heat."

"Aye," she said, letting him lead her to the Christmas crib as he held her close and they snuggled together beneath the cloak. Eva was in heaven once again.

CHAPTER 5

TURTLE DOVES AND PYGG JARS

*E*va awoke the next morning to hear pounding on her door.

"Who is it?" she called out, rolling over and snuggling into the warm covers. They reminded her of Sir Adam's warm cloak last night. They had snuggled together beneath his cloak as they watched the Christmas play and listened to the carolers. She had probably drunk too much mulled wine, but it felt good at the time even if her head hurt now. All she wanted to do was sleep.

"It's your handmaid, my lady. I'm here to help you dress," came the woman's muffled voice from the other side of the door.

"I don't need help today, but thank you," she called back, looking at the door from her prone position on the bed.

"Aye, my lady."

Eva caressed the pillow with her cheek pretending it was Adam's fingers against her skin. She had just closed her eyes again when the door banged open causing her to bolt upright.

"Grandmother, you scared me," she exclaimed, holding the blanket against her chest.

"What is the meaning of your laziness, Eva?"

"I'm just . . . tired today," she answered with a yawn.

"We'll see about that." The old woman shut the door, hobbled over and pulled open the shutter. Cold, crisp air as well as snow blew in, making Eva shiver.

"Close the shutter, Grandmother. I'm cold."

"I'll bet you'd like to be warm the way you were with Sir Adam fondling you under his cloak right in front of the baby Jesus in the manger last night."

"What?" That got her attention. Her eyes sprang open wide and she bolted off the bed. "That's a lie! There was no fondling going on. He only offered to share his cloak with me because I was cold."

"There is whispering through the rushes this morning that more than just cuddling happened between you two. Is this true?"

"Nay! It's not true at all." Eva quickly started to dress. "Tell me who is gossiping about me so I can rip out their tongues."

"I overheard some of the servants talking in the kitchen."

"Then I'll have them all flayed." Eva's blood boiled.

ELIZABETH ROSE

"There's no time for that. Have you written the missive
to the king yet to keep him from coming here on Twelfth
Night?"

"Nay, I haven't had time."

"Then make time," snapped the old woman. "Your
father will never be able to carry on a conversation with
the king. As soon as Edward realizes that Albert is not only
lame but addled, he'll snatch away his title, the castle and
his lands so fast that we're all going to end up on our rears
out in the cold snow."

"I'll do it, don't worry," she assured her grandmother. "I
won't let the king take away everything from us, I
promise."

"Then you'd better start thinking more about
protecting your father and his assets and stop thinking so
much about that silver-tongued devil, Sir Adam. He's going
to be our demise."

"Silver-tongued devil? I thought you liked Sir Adam
and said he was charming."

"He had me fooled at first, but not anymore."

"Don't worry, Grandmother. I will not let Sir Adam
distract me again. As soon as the meal is over I will write
that missive and send a messenger to deliver it to the king."

"Don't wait too long or it'll be too late," snapped the old
woman. "And whatever you do, don't lose your heart to Sir
Adam because it'll only hurt you in the end."

"I won't," Eva promised, knowing it was already too late
because she had already lost her heart to the mysterious
man.

* * *

"So what have you found out about her father?" Bryce asked as Adam leaned over the hearth stirring the kettle of bubbling frumenty. The hot porridge made of cracked wheat, eggs, slivered almonds, and sugar, was a staple food and called pottage. Adam dipped in a spoon to have a taste.

"I haven't found anything yet," he said. "I've been too busy in the kitchen to investigate matters further." Adam licked his lips and made a face. "Hand me that jar of cinnamon, Squire. This needs a little more spice."

Bryce handed him the jar. "You'll never be made a baron if you can't carry out this mission."

Adam snatched the jar from his hand and sprinkled it into the porridge. "You don't need to remind me. I am going to do it, but I wanted to make sure I won Lady Eva over first."

"I'm sure you did that last night. After all, everyone is talking about the two of you getting cozy together under your cloak."

"Nothing happened," said Adam, lifting the spoon to his squire's mouth. "Taste this. Does it need more almond milk or perhaps a little more meat broth?"

"You used both?" asked Bryce, since usually only one or the other was used in the preparation.

"Don't question me, just taste. Something is missing but I don't know what."

Bryce tasted it and nodded. "That's good. I'm glad you

didn't put those nasty currants in this time. I don't like them."

"Currants, that's it! That's what I forgot. Thank you, Bryce," said Adam, slapping his squire on the back. "I don't know where my mind is today."

"I do," mumbled Bryce under his breath.

"Take the pigeon pies out of the oven or they'll over-cook," Adam called out to the servants.

"We forgot about using these," called out a servant boy, holding up a cage with two turtle doves in it that Adam had saved from the butcher's block earlier.

"Nay! Put them down. Those aren't for eating," he called out.

"Sir Adam," Bryce tried to talk once again, but when a shrill voice called out from the other side of the kitchen, Adam's head popped up and his attention was diverted once again.

"It's Eva and she looks madder than all hell," said Adam, feeling affected by her presence, although he wasn't sure if it was good or bad.

"Was it you?" Eva grabbed a young servant boy by the front of his tunic and squeezed tightly.

"Nay, my lady, it wasn't me, I swear," squeaked out the boy in fear.

"Then how about you or you?" Eva dropped the boy and pointed an accusing finger at two more of the cooks. Her other hand was balled up and jammed up against her waist.

"It wasn't us, my lady, please don't hurt us," said one of the servant girls.

"Bid the devil, what is she doing?" Adam threw down the spoon and rushed across the room. "My lady, is there a problem with the servants?" he asked, noticing the mean look in her eyes. He hadn't seen this look since Christmas Eve when he tried to enter her castle uninvited.

"Someone here is spreading gossip about me and I don't like it!"

"Gossip?" Adam chuckled. "Whatever do you mean?"

"She's talking about the gossip about you fondling her under the cloak in front of the manger," said Bryce, biting into an apple as he came up alongside Adam.

"Squire, I don't need your help," growled Adam.

"Did you start the gossip?" Eva glared at Bryce. Both her hands were on her hips now.

"Me?" Bryce swallowed hard, almost choking on the apple in the process. His face turned white. "I only told the servants what Adam told me."

"What did you tell him?" Now Eva was shooting daggers from her eyes at Adam.

"My lady, please," said Adam, trying to calm her down. "I only told him that we shared my cloak and that I was fond of you."

"Fond?" Bryce made a face and the apple fell from his hand to the ground. "I thought you said you fondled her, not that you were fond of her," he told Adam under his breath.

"That, Squire, was your first mistake," said Adam. "And my mistake was telling you anything at all."

"I'm sorry, my lady, honest I am." Bryce talked to Eva as he backed away from her, and half-hid behind Adam. "I'll make sure all the servants know the truth."

"And the nobles," added Adam. "Don't forget to tell the nobles. After all, we don't want to sully Lady Eva's reputation."

"Aye, my lord," Bryce answered before turning and running off in the opposite direction.

"Your squire will be punished for that," snapped Eva.

"Now, why would you want to do that?" Adam scooped up a huge handful of dried currants from a barrel and walked over to the kettle and threw them into the pottage. "It was an honest mistake and he is going to correct it, so there is no harm done." He continued to stir the porridge.

"No harm done?" she squawked. "My reputation is on the line, if I must remind you."

Adam lifted a spoonful of pottage up to his mouth and nibbled at it. "Taste," he said, holding the wooden stirring spoon up to her mouth to distract her.

"What is it?" she asked, staring down her nose.

"It's frumenty with my secret ingredients added. That is, lots of cinnamon and nutmeg and a loving handful of currants."

"Currants? In the Christmas porridge?" Eva made a face and held out her hand. "I don't think I want any. I don't even like frumenty. I never have."

"Don't scrunch up your nose before you've even had a taste."

Without waiting for her to resist, Adam brought the spoon to his mouth, blowing on the mixture to cool it, and then stuck the tip of the spoon into her mouth.

EVA LIKED the intimacy of Adam blowing on her food. She opened her mouth willingly and let the spoon enter. The sweet taste of cinnamon exploded on her tongue mixed with the chewiness of the currants. It made a wonderful combination.

"It's good," she admitted, licking her lips. She noticed him staring at her lips. Then he took a step closer, still focused on her mouth. She was afraid he was going to kiss her again, so she quickly stepped backwards. When she moved, she stumbled and fell against the table where two birds in a cage started fussing and beating their wings against the bars. "What is the meaning of this?" she spat.

"That is Adam and Eve. They are a present for you, my lady. Those are two of the most perfect turtle doves you'll ever see because they are in love." He picked up the cage and handed it to her.

"For me?" she asked in question. No one had ever given her a gift like this before. "And you named them?"

"Aye. After us," he said with a smile. "Of course, since Adam and Eve were the very first couple, I called the bird Eve instead of Eva. I hope you don't mind."

"I've never had a bird named after me before." Her heart swelled from Adam's thoughtfulness.

"Go ahead and put your finger up to the cage and pet them," Adam urged her. "They'll coo. They like that."

"Oh, I don't know," she said, wringing her hands in front of her as she looked at the birds.

"Allow me." He took her hand in his. Their eyes interlocked and she felt heat engulf her. Then, guiding her, she petted the birds through the bars, while he held her hand.

Eva liked the way the birds rubbed up against her finger, but what she liked more was Adam holding her hand. She smiled, feeling as if she wanted to kiss him. Then she remembered her grandmother's warning and slowly pulled her hand out of his.

"What is that wonderful aroma?" she asked, trying to change the subject.

"Oh, that's part of our meal," Sir Adam told her. "I hope you like pigeon pie."

Her eyes flashed back to the doves that were cooing and rubbing up against each other. Adam and Eve, he'd called them. Lovers that were oblivious to the fact they had almost been part of the meal. Suddenly, she wasn't hungry.

* * *

AFTER THE MEAL WAS COMPLETED, Sir Adam hurried from the kitchen to talk to Eva before she left the great hall.

"My lady," he said, rushing after her, hoping to get her attention.

"What is it, Sir Adam? I have things to do." She continued to walk as she spoke.

"It'll only take a moment. Since it is St. Stephen's Day, I'm sure you'll want to give the servants the rest of the day off."

"What?" She stopped dead in her tracks and spun around. "Nay, I'd never do that. Why would I?"

"It's custom to let the servants take some of the leftover Christmas food and spend the day with their families."

"Aye, my lady," said her steward, Sir Geoffrey, over-hearing their conversation. He wandered over to join them. "I'm sorry to intervene, but what Sir Adam says is true. Your father always gives the servants the day off and sends them home with a gift as well on the feast of Saint Stephen. I'm surprised the earl hasn't told you. I'll go speak to him about it at once."

"Nay," she said, not wanting the steward to go to her father's solar. "I'm sure it'll be fine. Go ahead, Sir Geoffrey. Tell the servants to take the rest of the day for themselves."

"What about a gift?" asked the steward. "The earl always gives them a gift for their family. I'll go to his solar and ask –"

"Nay! Do not disturb my father. His leg is troubling him and he is sleeping. The church already opened the box of alms this morning, passing them out to the poor. That is enough of a gift."

"But I haven't spoken to the earl in six months now, my lady," said the steward. "There are things I need to discuss with him."

"Six months," repeated Adam. "And still, his leg isn't healed after all this time?"

Eva didn't want Adam asking any more questions, and neither did she want to leave him alone with Sir Geoffrey. That would be a recipe for trouble. She had been headed to her chamber to write the missive to the king, but now she would have to do it later. More important at the moment, she had to distract Adam.

"Sir Adam, what do you suggest we give the servants as a gift?"

His attention was diverted. Her plan worked. "Well," he said, holding his hand to his chin in thought. "I've been meaning to tell you that I checked the supply of goods in the undercroft."

"Good. I hope you found what you needed," she told him.

"I found many things including some exotic dried herbs and spices that I'll be using in the preparation of the meals. However, I also found a box with dozens of pyggs in it."

"Pyggs," repeated Eva, almost forgetting about the small clay pots with slits at the top that were made from orange clay called pygg. Oftentimes, when a servant was tossed a coin by a noble, they placed it into their pygg jar for safe keeping. Her mother used to put a pence in each and give them out to the servants at Christmastime. "Aye, we'll use those as gifts, Sir Adam." She turned back to her steward. "I'll get a bag of coins and you both can help me fill the pyggs and hand them out to the servants as they leave to spend the day with their families."

"That's a very thoughtful idea," said Adam with a smile that could melt her heart.

It wasn't easy trying to forget the man when he smiled at her in a manner that made her go weak in the knees.

CHAPTER 6

FRENCH HENS, COLLIE BIRDS AND HOLY INNOCENTS

*E*va had no idea where the time had gone. Yesterday, when the servants returned from their day off, Adam had surprised her by taking her out into the courtyard where they proceeded to hang apples from the bare branches of the trees in the castle orchard. He had reminded her that it had been Adam and Eve Day on Christmas Eve and hanging apples from the trees was a tradition.

She had known about it, but since her mother had passed away, a lot of the Christmastide traditions had been ignored or forgotten.

Adam had also insisted on taking her for a ride in the wagon to the coast where the trade ships had just come in to dock. There, they went from ship to ship buying not only soft velvet to make a new gown for her, but also bought herbs from faraway places. On the way back, Adam stopped in the churchyard where they purchased and consumed a good amount of Church Ale. This was a strong brew reserved and sold only at Christmastime.

Eva already felt dizzy by the time they returned to the castle. Adam decided she needed to eat and so he had prepared French hens brushed in garlic and basted with butter. They were filled with a breaded stuffing combined with onions, rosemary, and lavender.

She had been so satisfied that she went back to her chamber and fell asleep early. But today was the Feast Day of the Holy Innocents. This was a day that no one looked forward to. It was considered a day of bad luck since it was the day that Herod killed the boy babies looking for the baby Jesus. Even kings refused to be crowned on this day.

Eva approached her father's solar, hoping not to find her grandmother there. She still hadn't written the fake missive to the king, and the more time that passed, the harder it was becoming to do it.

"Father?" She poked her head into the room, gasping when she saw Adam and his squire standing at her father's bedside. The healer was there with them.

"What are you doing in here?" she spat, hurrying over to them. "Healer, didn't I tell you that no one was to disturb my father?"

"Aye, you did my lady," said the healer with a bow. "I'm sorry."

"It's not his fault," said Adam, holding a jar of some kind of ointment. "I insisted on seeing the earl.

"Who is it?" The earl opened his eyes and tried to lift his head. "Mother?" asked the confused man.

"Mother?" Adam looked at the earl oddly.

"He's having a dream about my mother, that's all." Eva pushed her way between Adam and the bed. "You'll have to leave now. He needs his rest."

"Wait," said Adam as she tried to send him away. "I wanted to show the healer the balm I made from comfrey, olive oil, and beeswax. It should help with healing your father's injured leg. Comfrey is wonderful with healing wounds and even sprains and broken bones." He held up the jar to show her.

"That's fine, thank you." Eva took the jar and left it on the table as she escorted Adam and Bryce to the door. "Today is the Feast Day of the Holy Innocents and there is much to be done. I'll not have you wasting another moment, Sir Adam."

ADAM HADN'T BEEN in the room with the earl for more than a few minutes before Eva barged in and hauled him away. He was never going to be able to complete his mission and find out if the earl was purposely ignoring the king if he wasn't allowed a minute to talk to the man. Something was odd here and he needed to look more carefully into the situation.

If it had been six months and still the earl's leg wasn't healed, then someone had to be lying. Adam had broken his leg when he was a youngster and it had been healed in just a few months. Even though the earl was old, in six months he should be up and walking again and not lying in bed calling other men Mother.

"We need to go out to the courtyard at once where the Boy Bishop will be chosen," Eva told him.

They all walked outside where a priest had chosen a youngster from the choir to act as Boy Bishop for the day. The boy was about ten years of age. He was immediately dressed in a mock bishop's robe, and given a mitre, or tall hat, as well as a staff with a cross at the top called a crozier.

"All the young boys, line up at once," called out one of the soldiers. Mothers cried and held on to their sons as the soldiers tried to pull them out of their hands. Blaxton, the gruffest, most relentless soldier at the castle walked to the front of the line with a whip in his hand.

"What's going on?" asked Adam, not liking the looks of this.

"It's Childermass," stated Eva. "Surely, you know that."

"Aye, I know that it is the Feast Day of the Holy Innocents and custom for the children to be beaten in their beds as a reminder of what Herod did but, surely, you aren't going to allow a soldier to whip them?"

"I have never liked this custom, Sir Adam," she told him, feeling a knot in her stomach. "However, you know as well as I that we cannot break the age-old custom, even though I don't like it one bit."

"Do something to stop it," stated Adam.

"I can't," she said with a trembling voice. "My father is the only one who can do that."

"Then someone get him."

63

"He is ill and cannot leave his bed. Besides, he will not break custom."

"Stop!" Adam shouted to the guard with a raised hand. "Eva, your father needs to be confronted about this. If you don't agree with it, then tell him so. Make him change his mind."

If Adam wasn't mistaken, he saw tears in Eva's eyes. He didn't understand her reaction, or why she didn't go to her father and get him to change his decision. It was frustrating him.

"My lady, you know this is custom and what we do every time on the Feast Day of the Holy Innocents. Everyone does it," said Blaxton, cracking his whip in the air. The children cried and the women screamed.

"Nay!" Eva cried out, boldly stepping up to the guard and snatching the whip out of his hand. A tear dripped down her cheek. "Sir Adam is right. No one will hurt these children today or any day from now on, no matter if it is custom or not."

"You don't have the authority to stop this," complained the guard.

"Get the earl," someone else shouted.

Lady Barbara walked forward with a folded up parchment in her hands. Her cane thumped against the ground with each step she took. "The earl is not able to join us today but while at his bedside he asked me to bring this missive. It states that within the walls of Cavendish Castle, there will no longer be the custom of hurting the children on the Feast Day of the Holy Innocents."

"Read the missive aloud," called out one of the guards.

Adam noticed the frightened look that flashed between Eva and her grandmother.

"Let's see that missive," growled Blaxton, reaching for the parchment.

Lady Barbara pulled it away and hit the soldier with her cane.

"I don't believe that missive is from the earl," said one of the knights.

"I don't believe it says anything at all," shouted someone else.

The crowd was in an uproar, all shouting out to see the missive. Adam saw despair and fear in Eva's eyes. Finally, she walked over and took the missive from her grandmother.

"I will read the missive aloud," she stated. "And then, if I hear anyone say another word that they don't believe my grandmother, they will be thrown into the dungeon for disrespect."

Eva's hands shook as she stepped back and opened the parchment, holding it close to her chest as she began to read.

"I, the earl of Cavendish of sound . . . mind and body . . . declare that the tradition of beating the children –" She swallowed hard and tried to blink a tear away from her eye. Adam didn't believe it either that the missive was from the earl. So he slipped back into the crowd and slowly made his way to sneak up behind her.

"Of beating the children," she continued. "It will no

longer be allowed."

"He can't do that," shouted one of the guards. "Only the king can give that order."

"Line up the boys," growled Blaxton, snapping his whip in the air, meaning to continue with the beating.

Adam peeked around several people, trying to see what was written on the parchment. And sure enough, just as he thought, the parchment was blank. The earl hadn't given the order, and neither had he written a missive at all. Things looked to be going from bad to worse on this unlucky day. He had to do something quickly to help Eva.

Slinking back into the crowd, Adam made his way quickly over to the newly chosen Boy Bishop.

EVA FRANTICALLY LOOKED around at the angry and frightened faces of the crowd feeling as if things had gotten out of hand. While she didn't want the children harmed, it was true that it was tradition and the king or the church were the only ones who could change it. Unfortunately, her attempt to fake an order from her father didn't matter in the least.

She frantically looked around for Adam, wanting his support. To her dismay, he was nowhere to be found. Then she finally spotted him over by the well, talking to the Boy Bishop whose name was Timothy. Anger boiled within her that when she needed him the most, he disappeared to talk to a child.

"Line up the first one," said Blaxton with a grunt. A

guard grabbed a little boy of about five years of age and held one arm while another guard took the other. The boy cried and his mother screamed from behind him.

This couldn't happen. Eva wouldn't allow it. Running forward, she darted in front of the boy, pulling the child into her embrace just as the whip came down. She bravely took the lash to her back in place of the child.

When it hit her body, Eva cringed, trying hard to hold back the shout threatening to spill forth from her mouth. The sting was unbearable, bringing tears to her eyes.

"Stop!" shouted Adam, coming forward with Timothy at his side. "The Boy Bishop is in charge today and makes all the decisions."

"He can't stop an age-old tradition," growled Blaxton.

"Mayhap not, but he certainly can change it," replied Adam. "Timothy, go ahead and tell everyone your decision about the beating of the children on the Feast Day of the Holy Innocents."

The boy stepped forward and started to speak, but the crowd became restless.

"We can't hear him," shouted someone from the back of the crowd.

"We can't see him," yelled someone else.

"Up you go, Timmy," said Adam, raising the boy up onto his shoulder. "How's that?" yelled Adam.

"Go ahead, Timmy," said Eva with a tremble to her voice. "And be sure to speak up so everyone can hear you."

Adam was ready to draw his sword and strike down the fool who ripped Eva's gown and made her bleed with his whip. Yet, he said nothing, because Eva's heroic action would gain her respect amongst the servants and peasants and he didn't want to take that away from her.

Timmy looked out at the crowd and talked as loudly as he could. "As Boy Bishop of the day, I declare that instead of the children being beaten or whipped, Sir Adam will tickle each of them until they beg for mercy."

The guards grumbled and the mothers of the children sighed in relief. The knights laughed heartily as this announcement.

"You heard him," said Adam, putting the boy on the ground. "Now, all boys line up in front of me and don't waste any time. Who is first?"

The rush of children to Adam was so overwhelming, that he almost fell to the ground. Then one by one, he took each of the boys and tickled them until they could laugh no more. Finally, when it was all over, he made his way to Eva and pulled her into his arms.

"Are you all right?" he asked, pushing a strand of hair behind her ear.

"I am now that you saved the children from being hurt." She wiped a tear from her eye. "Thank you, Adam."

"Let me see your wound." He turned her around to look at the rip in her gown. A red, raised welt from the whip was showing against her skin. "I'll kill that bastard for hurting you," he said with a clenched jaw.

"Nay, don't, Adam. The guard was only doing his job. But I thank you for stepping in to help the children. You are amazing."

To Adam's surprise, Eva reached up and gave him a peck on the cheek.

"You are the one who sacrificed yourself to help them," he said, pulling her into his arms. "You should feel proud of what you did."

Her long lashes blinked away more tears. "I think I'll see the healer now and then take a long bath before the meal."

"Be sure to have the healer use my comfrey salve on you," he told her. "And by the way, I've talked to Timmy. Since he makes the decisions on this day, he's told me what he wants to eat."

"What's that?" she asked, flashing a small smile.

"He said he wants a Collie Bird pie."

"Collie Bird? Oh, Adam, that sounds terrible," Eva said with a groan, thinking about the hideous blackbirds. Those calling birds always woke her in the mornings when all she wanted to do was sleep.

"Don't worry, I have something planned that will please everyone," Adam assured her. "Now, hurry and get cleaned up because I'll have a feast waiting for you when you return."

* * *

Two hours later, Eva was feeling much better. After soaking in a bath and changing her clothes, she felt like a new woman. Actually, it was the comfrey salve that Adam had given the healer that gave her the most relief. In just that short time, her skin was already beginning to heal.

She sat at the dais alongside her father and grand-mother as well as the Boy Bishop, awaiting Adam's promised surprise. Since her father had awoken and his fever broke, she decided she should bring him down to the great hall to be seen by his people. Too many were becoming suspicious, and she had to assure them that her father was still of sound mind and body and capable of ruling Cavendish, even if he wasn't.

The food procession started, and the music resounded though the great hall. To her surprise, Adam led the line, carrying a large pie in his hands. Her stomach clenched already. She didn't want to eat blackbirds. It didn't sound at all appealing.

"My lady," said Adam. "Here is the Collie Bird pie that's been requested by the Boy Bishop."

"Aye," said Timmy excitedly, getting up on his knees on the chair to get a better view of the pie. It was huge and covered with a crust on top that barely looked cooked. The pie itself was lumpy and she swore the wretched-looking thing was moving.

"My lady, will you please cut the pie?" Adam laid the pie in front of her. Hilt first, he handed her a dull knife, resting it over his arm.

"Nay, I don't want to do it," she said, shaking her head and lifting a hand in the air to ward him away.

"Then allow me to do it for you," said Adam, turning the knife around. He lifted up the pie to let everyone in the great hall see it. Then he turned back to Eva and carefully and slowly, tapped the top of the crust with the flat end of the knife. When the crust was broken, Eva jumped back in alarm and held her hand to her heart. To her surprise, live blackbirds flew out of the pie and headed up to land in the rafters.

She was shocked, relieved, and amazed, all at the same time. Breaking loose with all her emotions she had been holding back lately, she laughed harder than she ever had in her life.

"Sir Adam, you are the best cook we've ever had at Cavendish and I admire you and everything you do," she told Adam.

"Thank you, my lady." Adam put down the empty pie shell and knife and reached out for her. "Thank you, very much." He kissed the back of her hand, letting the kiss linger. And then he looked up into her eyes and smiled right before he kissed her hand again, letting his tongue shoot out to lick her.

"Oh!" she exclaimed, looking around nervously, hoping no one saw him. Her father laughed heartily at the birds and slapped his left hand atop the table. Timmy stood on the chair with his arms over his head trying to reach the birds. Even her grandmother had a grin on her face.

Eva's eyes met Adam's and within his gaze she felt as if she'd truly lost her heart to him now. This was only the fourth day of Christmas, but she was already dreading Twelfth Night when he would step out of her kitchen and leave her life forever. That, she didn't think she could ever bear.

CHAPTER 7

GOLDEN RINGS, GEESE AND SWANS

The next three days were a blur to Eva. She had been spending more and more time with Sir Adam and every day seemed to be more memorable than the last. He went out of his way to please her, not only with food, but also by treating her honorably, as Lady of the Castle.

Adam escorted her to church each day, and even to town to check on the tenants. They spent time riding in the brisk, cool air, and he even walked with her atop the battlements when she checked on the garrison to make sure things were in order.

Everyone was happier than ever this Yuletide season, and she had Sir Adam to thank for it all. Not since her mother was alive had the food tasted so delicious. She only wished her father's health would improve because Twelfth Night was approaching quickly and the king would be here before she knew it.

"Do you have that missive written yet to the king?" asked her grandmother from the other side of Eva's bedchamber.

"I'm not sure what to write." Eva stared at the blank parchment in front of her as she held a feather quill in her hand. The bottle of ink sat on the table but she had yet to use it.

"Tell him that it isn't advisable that he comes to Cavendish at this time," said Lady Barbara, staring out the open window. "Make up something. Use me as an excuse if you have to, but do it. You can tell him I've come down with a horrible illness and the healer doesn't think the king should come near for fear he'll be stricken with it as well."

"I don't know," said Eva, tapping the end of the quill on the table in thought. "I don't want to keep lying, Grandmother. What if the king finds out there is nothing wrong with you? Suppose he summons our healer."

"That is why we pay the healer large sums of money," said Lady Barbara. "To keep his mouth shut. Now, don't wait another minute or it'll be too late. Write the missive at once and send a messenger to the king so it'll stop him from showing up at our doorstep in a sennight."

"It doesn't feel right." Eva put down the quill. "Mayhap there is another way to save Father from being stripped of his title and to save his castle and lands."

"You know as well as I that the king won't have an earl who cannot even lift a sword." Lady Barbara closed the shutter. "My son will be demoralized and lose everything. Do you want that to happen to your father as well as us?

We'll end up living like paupers in a shack made of wattle and daub before this is all over."

"I suppose you're right. We can't have that." Eva sighed and picked up her quill and dipped it into the ink. "I'll write the missive and send it to the king."

"That's good," said Lady Barbara, thumping her cane against the floor as she hobbled to the door. "I am going to check on your father. He has been asking to join in the festivities – or at least I think that's what he's saying. Between his slurred speech and his addlepated comments lately, I'm not sure what he wants."

"All right, Grandmother. I'll be there later."

As soon as her grandmother left, Eva wrote the missive that she really didn't want to write. After she finished, she blew on the ink to dry it and read it over silently to herself. She would have to find the messenger and send the missive off to the king without further delay.

"Lady Eva?" came a deep voice from the door.

She looked up in surprise to see Adam peeking into the room though he still stood in the corridor.

"Sir Adam! What are you doing here?"

"I knocked several times but I guess you didn't hear me. May I come in?"

"I – of course," she said, hurriedly folding the parchment and depositing it into the small chest atop the table, slamming down the lid. She didn't have time to seal the missive with wax and stamp it with the earl's signet ring, but she would attend to that later.

"Oh, I see you were busy writing." Adam sauntered into

the room, seeming very curious as to what she was doing. "Whom were you writing to?"

"It's not important," she said, jumping up from her chair. "What was it you wanted?" Eva purposely stood in front of the chest, blocking his view with her body.

"I came to escort you to the wassailing that will start in the orchard momentarily." His eyes seemed to be focused on the table behind her.

"Aye, let's go. My cloak is on the hook if you'd be kind enough to get it for me."

"Of course, my lady," he said with a slight bow. He retrieved the cloak and headed back to help her don it. "We'll have to stop in the great hall first where the Wassail King and Queen will be chosen by the Lord of Misrule to lead the procession."

"Of course," she said, seeing him eye the table with the missive once more before they headed out the door.

As soon as they got down to the great hall, Adam left Eva for a moment, making his way through the crowd to talk to his squire.

"Bryce," he said, pulling his squire aside. The boy had been singing and dancing and, of course, drinking and flirting with the lovely ladies in the room.

"What is it?" asked Bryce, walking over and dipping his wooden cup into the large wassail bowl to refill it. Wassail was a hot cider mixed with wine. The drink was infused with spices such as cinnamon, ginger, and nutmeg, and had roasted crab apples floating atop it. Around the large bowl on the table were sops, or toasted pieces of bread that were normally soaked in the liquid and then eaten.

"Did you pay the Lord of Misrule the money so he will choose Lady Eva and myself as the Queen and King of the Wassail?" he asked.

"Aye, I certainly did, my lord." Bryce brought the cup to his mouth, took a sip, and smacked his lips in satisfaction. "Did you find out anything yet about the –" he leaned in closer and whispered. "The mission?"

Adam smelled whisky on the boy's breath. It was obvious his squire had been spiking the wassail bowl.

"Mayhap," he answered. "I found out the earl never wrote a missive on the Feast Day of the Holy Innocents. The parchment was blank. And I also caught Lady Eva writing a missive in her chamber just now. I was going to ask you to sneak in and read it. But in your condition, I think it best that I do the job myself."

"To your health," said Bryce with a huge smile, lifting his cup in the air and staggering back a step.

The straight trumpet sounded and the Lord of Misrule jumped up onto a bench and raised his hand in the air to get everyone's attention. Adam hurried back to Eva's side.

"And now, for the choosing of the King and Queen of the Wassail," said the boy. "I choose Lady Eva and Sir Adam."

The crowd cheered and clapped.

"Me?" asked Eva, seeming shocked by the announcement. "Nay, choose someone else."

"Nonsense, my lady. You'll make a fine Queen of the Wassail." Adam took her by the arm and escorted her to the front of the processional line.

"Nay, Adam. I don't think I should. My father believes this is a pagan custom and he wouldn't like it if he knew that I was acting as queen of the celebration."

"Then we won't tell him, will we?" Adam dipped a wooden cup into the wassail bowl, placing a sop on top. Then he took hold of her arm. "To the orchard, my good queen, where we will pay homage to the apple trees to awaken them, and sing and dance to scare away the evil spirits. Then, there will be no doubt that next year you'll have a good harvest."

"I still don't think this is a good idea," she mumbled as he led her to the door.

"You'll ride with me, my queen," he said, escorting her to the stable.

"Ride? Where are we going?" she asked in confusion. "The orchard is inside the castle walls."

"Aye, but today we're going to celebrate in your father's larger orchard outside the walls. The villeins and serfs will join us."

After a short ride to the orchard, the singing and dancing began. Adam dismounted, holding on to the cup of wassail as he helped her dismount. The musicians had followed and the serfs and villeins came out of their houses to join in the celebration. Everyone lined up at the back of a wagon where the servants served them wassail from a large wooden tub.

"Have some wassail and loosen up, my lady," said Adam, bringing the cup to her mouth. He didn't tell her that Bryce had spiked the wassail bowl, but she didn't need to know. After much drinking of the wassail, singing and dancing around the trees, as was custom, Adam lifted Eva up into the branches of one of the apple trees.

"Put me down," she said, laughing because of all the wassail she'd drunk. "What are you doing?"

"You know as well as I that the Wassail Queen must place a piece of toast that's been dipped in wassail into the tree as an offering. He handed her the soggy piece of bread from his cup.

"Oh, all right," she said, reaching up to place the bread in the boughs of the tree. Someone recited a fertility incantation and then the music started up again as the procession headed back to the castle. "Can I come down from here now?" asked Eva.

"Of course, my queen." Adam took her in his arms and held her off the ground with her head on one side and her feet on the other.

"I'm not a queen, so stop saying that," she told him.

"You are queen for the day and will forever be a queen in my eyes." He held her in his arms, staring into her beautiful eyes.

"You can release me now," she said, gazing into his eyes as well and doing nothing to try to get free.

"Not yet," he told her, bending over, pressing his lips up against hers.

. . .

EVA'S HEAD spun and she felt very dizzy as Adam touched his lips to hers in a sensuous, sweet kiss. He tasted like cinnamon, apples, and if she wasn't mistaken . . . whisky. She liked the kiss and no longer cared that someone might be watching and start gossip about them. Feeling relaxed from the wassail and happy for being with Adam, she wrapped her arms around his neck and kissed him in return.

"Mayhap, we shouldn't have kissed," she said shyly. "I mean, there is no kissing bough hanging over our heads."

Adam's eyes flashed upward. "Does a sop of wassail bread count?" he asked with a chuckle.

"I don't think so. Kissing is only allowed under the mistletoe."

"Well, my lady, you are my mistletoe, and always will be. So I supposed it counts after all."

"If you say so," she answered with a giggle. "And you are my chain mail."

"Chain mail? Is that your new pet name for me now?"

"You were wearing chain mail when I first met you," she reminded him. "And since you called me Mistletoe, I think it is only fair I call you Chain Mail in return."

"Fair enough," he said, kissing her once more before gently placing her on her feet. "Now, we're off to the great hall where I've prepared another feast in your honor. It is New Year's Eve, my lady, and I have a remarkable surprise in store for you."

"What more could you possibly cook?" Eva asked as they headed to the horse. "You've already amazed me by creating those outstanding golden rings of Bryndon." Eva's mouth watered just thinking of the fried rings of cake filled with figs, dates, and pine nuts. The cakes were colored with saffron to make them look gold, and drizzled with wine and honey.

"Was the Bryndon to your liking?" he asked, lifting her into the saddle.

"It was. And so was the meal of goose filled with the delicious stuffing of grapes, garlic, cider vinegar, and parsley. Just thinking about it makes me hungry. Sir Adam, I never knew a knight could be such a fine cook, let alone a cook at all."

"You have no idea of all the wonderful secret recipes I have collected throughout the years."

"I will miss your cooking when you leave."

"Is that all you'll miss?" he asked, pressing his mouth up to her ear and nibbling on her lobe.

"I'll miss not only your cooking but also you, Sir Adam. I wish you didn't have to go. By the way, you never told me where you live."

"Let's just say I live in the moment and leave it at that."

As they rode back to the castle, Eva wondered what Adam meant by that.

The meal that night was delicious as always, making Eva crave the presence of Sir Adam even more. He had served swan and it was the most amazing thing she'd ever seen. After cooking the bird, he had reattached all the feathers. He presented the swan to her in its most glorious form with its huge wings spread out as if in flight. She didn't know how he managed to do it.

The great hall was decorated with many lit candles inside as well as out in the courtyard, since it was tradition to light the candles to guide the departed souls to the other side. There was also an empty trencher set at the dais on New Year's Eve, symbolizing a place being set for the loved ones who had departed throughout the year.

"Did you send out the missive?" Lady Barbara leaned over and whispered into Eva's ear. The earl wasn't at the celebration tonight. His health had taken another turn for the worse and the healer was watching over him.

"Nay, not yet," she whispered back, talking into her cup as she took a drink of wine.

"Why not?" complained her grandmother. "You are letting that wretched knight distract you and I don't like it."

Eva looked down to her trencher, pushing the Pescodde around with her spoon. She loved the taste of the peas and bacon, but her grandmother's angry persistence made her stomach turn in a knot.

"I will do it when I get around to it," she snapped. "And I'll kindly ask you not to call Sir Adam wretched. He is the best thing that has happened around here in a long time."

"He's using you, but you are too blind to see it."

Eva's head jerked upward. "How can you say that? He has been nothing but kind and accommodating to me."

"I don't like him. There is something he is hiding and I will get to the bottom of it if it's the last thing I ever do."

"Leave well enough alone, Grandmother."

"Nothing is well. Certainly not your father. But you don't care about that, do you? All you care about is that knight who is seducing you through your stomach. If you didn't like food so much, it wouldn't be a problem."

"Stop it!" Eva sprang out of her chair just as Adam approached the dais with a platter of freshly baked mince pies in his hand. They were made from minced pork and beef as well as currants, figs, and other dried fruits along with lots of cloves. This was one of Eva's favorite holiday dishes.

"My lady, where are you going?" asked Adam. His eyes darted to her grandmother and then back to her.

"I'm going to my chamber."

"But it's New Year's Eve," he said. "There is still a lot to come. Did you know the Irish bang on their walls to scare off evil spirits on this night? And the Scots call it Hogmanay, welcoming First Foot – the first person to step over the threshold after midnight. A dark-haired guest is considered good luck throughout the year."

"I don't care about traditions from Ireland or Scotland, so if you'll excuse me, Sir Adam, I am going to my chamber for the rest of the evening."

"But you've yet to eat of the mince pie." He picked up a palm-sized pie and held it out to her.

"I'm not hungry," she lied, glaring at her grandmother who made her feel fat.

"Lady Eva, it is bad luck not to eat of a mince pie offered to you. You don't want bad luck, do you?"

"Nay, I don't." She glanced at her grandmother once more when she said it. The woman was motioning with her eyes for Eva to leave to send out the missive. Eva didn't want to leave. She was enjoying the meal and enjoying Sir Adam's company even more. "You are right, Sir Adam. I will stay and eat my mince pie as is proper." She sat back down and brought the pie to her mouth, ignoring her grandmother's warning.

"Don't forget, you need to make a wish when you take a bite," Adam reminded her.

"I will." She released a breath, closed her eyes, and bit into the mince pie. Her wish was for her father to be healed and also for Sir Adam to stay at Cavendish Castle. Forever.

CHAPTER 8

MILKMAIDS AND THE FEAST OF FOOLS

*T*he next morning, Adam dressed as he spoke with Bryce. "Are you sure you understand what to do?" he asked, fastening his belt around his waist.

"Aye, my lord," said Bryce, sitting up on his pallet at the foot of Adam's bed. He stretched and yawned loudly.

"Well, let's hear it. I don't have much confidence you'll remember a thing today since you were so far in your cups last night."

"During the Feast of Fools, I am to dance with Lady Eva so you don't have to." He got up and blinked, holding on to the bedpost to remain steady.

"You're being the biggest fool of all," grumbled Adam, sitting down on the edge of the bed to don his boots. "It's not that I don't want to dance with her, it is so I can sneak away to check that missive in her chamber. Now, did you secure two costumes exactly the same for us, as well as hats and masks?"

"I did," said Bryce, heading over to a travel bag. "Let me show you."

"Good, good," mumbled Adam, hoping the disguise would fool Eva long enough so that she would think she was dancing with him instead of Bryce. Once he returned from his mission, he would take his proper place and his squire would slip away. Eva would have no idea of what happened.

"Here you are. Did you want to wear yours now?" Bryce held up a dress as well as a wimple.

"What the hell is that?" Adam growled, getting to his feet and narrowing his eyes as he surveyed the dress.

"It's the Feast of Fools," Bryce told him. "The men dress like women and the women dress like men. We will be dressed as milkmaids today. I even secured wimples," he said proudly, holding up a white wimple and then placing it over his head and dancing around like a wench.

"Ugh," said Adam, not wanting to dress up like a girl. He needed to get down to the kitchen and had no time to look for another costume to wear, so he had no other choice. "What about our masks?"

"Right here." Bryce dug into the bag and held up two eye masks that stopped just over the nose.

Adam sighed and shook his head. "Do you see a slight problem with that, Squire?"

"With what?" Bryce inspected the masks, holding one up to his eyes.

"This." Adam walked up and gently slapped Bryce's cheek.

"Ow! What was that for?" Bryce made a face and rubbed his cheek.

"You have no facial hair, Squire, and I do. Don't you think she'll notice?"

"Oh, you're right." Bryce rubbed his chin in thought. "I suppose I can try to come up with a fake beard. Perhaps I can sneak to the stable and steal some hair from the horses' manes."

"Don't bother." Adam walked over to the basin of water in the room and removed his dagger from his waist belt, holding it up to his cheek.

"What are you doing, my lord?" Bryce rubbed his eyes and yawned again.

"I am going to shave, you fool. If you don't have facial hair then neither can I or our plan will never work."

"Do you think she'll notice?" Bryce scratched his armpit, then burped aloud and continued to rub his fingers through his tangled hair.

"If she thinks you are me, I'll be insulted. But for the sake of the plan, let's hope she doesn't notice a thing."

EVA DRIPPED the wax onto the missive to seal it, picking up her father's signet ring with her other hand.

"I need to get to your father's solar," her grandmother announced, heading to the door. "He has been asking to join the festivities, although I am not sure he knows what he's saying. I figured we could dress him up and if he acts like a fool, it won't matter today. It's good for the rest of the castle to see him once in a while or they are going to get suspicious."

"People are already suspicious," said Eva, pressing the crest of the ring into the soft wax. "I don't know how much longer I can keep the steward from talking with Father. And I found Sir Adam by Father's bedside the other day asking the healer a lot of questions."

"You did?" Lady Barbara pursed her mouth. "I want Sir Adam out of here at once," snapped Lady Barbara.

"Nay, he has to stay and cook in the kitchen until Twelfth Night is over."

"Then if you don't kick him out after Twelfth Night, I will. Now, don't forget. Find the messenger and send that missive at once."

"Aye, Grandmother," said Eva, blowing on the wax to help it harden. Eva looked at the missive, feeling a knot in her stomach again. She had always done her grandmother's bidding since she didn't want to lose her home. Neither did she want her father to lose his title and lands. But how much longer could they keep up this charade? If the king discovered she was the one to forge her father's messages, what would happen to her? This could be considered treason and she might very well be punished. Would she go to the stocks or hang by her neck? She didn't want to die. But she did want to protect her father.

With one hand rubbing the back of her neck, she stared at the missive in her hand. Her grandmother wanted her to send it to the king. Part of her wanted to do so, but another part of her wanted to come out with the truth. She was confused and no longer knew what to do.

Before she had a chance to think about it any longer, a knock on her door jarred her from her thoughts.

"Who is it?" she called out.

"It's the milkmaid, my lady," answered someone who sounded like a man but with an odd, high voice.

"The milkmaid?" she said to herself, not understanding what she'd be doing at her door. Curious to know, she decided she needed to find out. Eva opened the lid to the chest and closed the missive inside. Then she picked up her skirts and hurried over and opened the door.

"Yes?" she asked, surveying the ugly, big-boned woman with drooping breasts. The stranger wore a wimple covering her head and a mask over her eyes.

"Can I escort you to the Feast of Fools?" asked the woman, her voice sounding oddly familiar. Eva looked down to see the gown stopped just past the woman's knees. She had very hairy legs and wore a pair of men's shoes. It wasn't a woman at all!

Eva started laughing. "Oh, nay, I'm afraid not. Sir Adam is escorting me to the Feast of Fools today."

"It's me," said Adam, raising his mask so she could see his face.

"It really is you." Eva reached out and ran her fingertips over his smooth cheek. "I thought you were handsome with the beard and mustache, but I like the clean-shaven look even better."

"Why aren't you ready to go?" Adam's eyes scanned down her body.

"I am ready."

"Where is your costume?"

"I will attend the festival, however, I will not wear a costume."

"Why not?"

"I'm sorry, Sir Adam, but I do not believe in such tomfoolery even if it is custom."

"Oh, so you don't like to deceive people by making them think you are someone else?"

His words cut her to the bone. Hadn't that been exactly what she'd been doing by pretending to be her father writing the missives to the king?

"No more questions, Sir Adam. If we are going to the Feast of Fools, then let us be off."

Glancing over her shoulder at the chest containing the missive, she figured she should go back and get it. But Adam's words kept ringing in her ears and she couldn't send it out today after what he'd just said. One more day wouldn't make a difference, she decided, and closed the door behind them.

ADAM ESCORTED Eva to the Feast of Fools where almost everyone was dressed in colorful, odd clothes. Men were dressed as women and women as men. Many looked like jesters. Everyone drank heartily of not only ale and wine but also of brandy and whisky.

Adam was quite proud of the feast he dished up today because even that was in disguise. He served Leche Lumbard which was a pork loaf formed into what looked like a gigantic peapod. Then he made up a dish of veal that resembled a sturgeon. But his all-time favorite ever since he was a boy was the Trayne Roste. This consisted of dried fruits and nuts threaded together on a string. It was then dipped in a beer batter and fried up to look like entrails. It was a very tasty treat.

"Lady Eva, I see your father is here and also wearing a costume. He seems so happy today. Perhaps he would like to participate in the egg games."

"His leg isn't healed yet, Sir Adam. I'm afraid he cannot."

"Nonsense. His chair has wheels," said Adam. "And all he'll have to do is balance an egg on a spoon as I wheel him to the other end of the great hall and back."

He raced off to get the earl, leaving Eva standing there alone. Adam heard her protests from behind him, but he didn't care. If he were going to get to the bottom of all this, he needed to talk to the earl. He purposely waited until Lady Barbara had walked away before he approached the man. The healer stood at his side with his hand on the back of the earl's chair. It was parked in a corner of the great hall.

"Earl Cavendish, can I interest you in joining in on the egg game today?" Adam stopped a servant carrying a bowl of eggs and plucked one up, as well as a spoon from the bowl.

"Egg game? I would love to join." The earl's voice sounded slurred as if he was already well in his cups.

"Oh, I'm afraid he can't," protested the healer, stepping forward to try to stop him. But Adam stepped around the man and pushed the earl's chair forward to join the line of others playing the game. The object was to race to the other side of the room and back, balancing an egg on a spoon. Whoever made it across the finish line first without dropping their egg was the winner.

"Sir Adam, release my father," commanded Eva, rushing up behind him. Adam kept wheeling the earl forward until they reached the starting line. "Sir Adam my father will not be playing this foolish game. Do you hear me?"

"I told him that, my lady," said the healer rushing after her, sounding very worried.

"Nonsense," said Adam. "Your father wants to play. He told me so himself."

"Healer, where is my grandmother?" asked Eva, urgency sounding in her tone. "She will put an end to this."

"She took a trip to the garderobe, my lady," said the healer. "Shall I go find her?"

"Don't bother. The earl will be finished with the game before she returns." Adam handed the spoon to the earl. "We're up next, Earl. Take this spoon and I'll balance the egg upon it."

"Nay, he doesn't want to play," protested Eva.

"Yes, I do," growled the earl.

. . .

Eva watched in horror as Adam handed her father the spoon. He held it out to her father's right hand, but of course her father couldn't take it.

"Here, take it," said Adam, picking up the man's hand and trying to put the spoon in it. When Adam realized the man couldn't hold it, his eyes snapped up to Eva's in question. She had to do something fast before everyone noticed he couldn't move his sword arm.

"It's an easy game, Father," said Eva, rushing forward and snatching the spoon away from Adam. "I think you'll enjoy it." She handed it to his left hand and her father took it. Then she reached out and retrieved the egg from Adam, balancing it on her father's spoon.

Adam stared at her with an open mouth. He looked so ridiculous dressed like a milkmaid and wearing the mask that she almost laughed. "Well, Milkmaid Adam, are you going to stand here gawking all day or are you going to push my father in the race?"

"Aye," replied Adam, clearing his throat and nodding his head. "Are you ready, Earl Cavendish?"

"I'm ready. Push me, wench! I want to win."

"Wench?" Adam scowled at her father.

"Go on, Milkmaid," said Eva with a chuckle, reaching out and straightening the lumps of clothes under his shirt that made up his breasts. Then she reached out and when no one was looking, she pinched him on the rear.

Adam jumped and lifted his mask, showing her his lusty

stare. "Do that again but when we're alone," he told her in a low voice.

The Lord of Misrule who was in charge of the games called out and the race began between the earl and another knight dressed like a jester.

"Hold on to that egg, Earl," said Adam, taking off at a run, pushing the man in his chair. He was neck and neck with the competition, but right at the end the knight dropped his egg and Adam went whizzing past with the earl, winning the race.

"I won!" called out the earl, making Eva's heart swell with joy. Her father's smile might be lopsided and his speech slurred, but he was happy for the first time in a long time.

"Father, you are the winner," said Eva, rushing over to take the egg and give her father a big hug.

"Here is your prize, my lord." Adam placed a silly-looking crown on the man's head that was made from greenery and looked a lot like one of the kissing boughs if Eva wasn't mistaken.

"Oh, look," said Adam pointing to a wide but shallow bowl filled with liquid. It was set atop the trestle table and there were flames coming from it.

"Fire!" called out her father.

"Don't worry, Father, it's just a game," Eva assured him, patting him on his shoulder.

"That's right," said Adam. "It's called Snapdragon. The object of the game is to snatch the flaming raisins out of the burning brandy, putting out the fire in your mouth as if you were a dragon."

"That's silly and dangerous," scoffed Eva.

"Nay, it's not." Adam shrugged his shoulders. "I have been playing this since I was a boy. Watch how it's done." Adam walked over to the bowl and snatched a raisin from the blue flames. He put it in his mouth, and Eva gasped, seeing his mouth on fire. Then he closed his mouth, made a face and swallowed. Opening his mouth to show her that it was gone, the crowd cheered for him. "See? It's easy," said Adam, walking back to her father's chair.

"I want to try it," said her father in his slurred speech.

"Nay, Father," said Eva. "Grandmother wouldn't allow it."

"What is this?" snapped her grandmother, storming up to them. "Healer, I told you to watch over him." She picked up her cane and knocked the healer over his head.

"I'm sorry, my lady," stuttered the healer. "But Sir Adam –"

"Sir Adam, you will stay away from the earl, and not bother him again. Do you understand?" Lady Barbara glared at Adam.

"Grandmother, Father is enjoying himself. There was no harm done," explained Eva.

"I want a flaming raisin," called out her father.

"What is this monstrosity on his head?" Lady Barbara flung the crown of greenery from the earl's head, causing him to shout out.

"Naaaaay, wench. Leave me be!"

Everyone turned to look at them and the music even stopped playing.

"Healer, wheel him up to his room at once. He shouldn't even be down here," ordered Lady Barbara.

"Grandmother, let him stay at the festival. He is enjoying himself," Eva pleaded with her.

Her grandmother glared in her direction. "I hope you did that little errand, Eva. Because if not, there is going to be hell to pay."

Lady Barbara and the healer left with the earl and the celebration started up once again.

"What little errand?" asked Adam.

"Nothing. It's not important," said Eva, watching her father being wheeled away. When the music started up again, Eva wanted nothing more than to be in Adam's arms. "Would you like to dance, Sir Adam?" she asked boldly, taking the chance that he wouldn't say no.

"I thought it was the man's prerogative to ask the woman," he said with a flash of white teeth.

"Well, since we are both looking like women tonight, I didn't think it made a difference." She held back a chuckle.

He made a face, but then nodded in agreement. "You're right. Just let me get a drink of ale to cool the fire in my mouth and I'll meet you by the Yule log for a dance in just a moment."

"I'll be waiting," she said, looking up at him shyly, hoping by the end of the night he'd kiss her again.

She loitered by the Yule log burning brightly on the hearth, wondering what was taking Adam so long. The room was very crowded and she didn't see him anywhere. Then, just as she was about to go look for him, she spied his hideous disguise in the crowd and waved at him.

"Sir Adam, here I am," she called out to him.

He wore his mask, but when he noticed her he came to her side.

"Is your mouth still on fire?" she asked playfully, grabbing his arm. "Because if so, perhaps we will share a hot, passionate kiss later under the kissing bough."

"Aye," he answered in a high squeak. Then he cleared his throat and said "Aye" in a much lower voice.

"Is something wrong with your voice?" she asked as they started the dance. "Did you burn your tongue on that flaming raisin?"

"What raisin?" he asked, sounding as if he truly didn't know what she was talking about.

They danced a little but he didn't hold her tightly like she expected. Instead, he kept his distance and seemed stiff and aloof. He wasn't acting like the friendly, chivalrous man he usually was when he was around her.

"That was nice what you did for my father," she said, trying to start up a conversation.

"Nice," he repeated, sounding like a fool. What was the matter with him? Had she done something to make him angry? She wanted to lighten up the situation and see him smile at her again. So the next time he turned, she moved closer. Hoping no one would see her, she pinched him playfully on the rear.

He turned so quickly that he stumbled. And when he

fell to the ground his mask went askew. Seeing more of his face, she realized that he wasn't Adam. Eva reached down and ripped off his mask, feeling like a fool.

"You're Sir Adam's squire," she retorted.

"I am," he said with a crooked smile. "Surprise, my lady."

"Sir Adam made me look like a fool." She put her hands on her hips.

"Well, it is Feast of Fools," he said, shrugging his shoulders.

"When you see Sir Adam, you can tell him that I don't think his jest was funny. And you can also tell him I'll not take part in this Feast of Fools another minute." She turned and stormed off.

"Wait!" cried Bryce, jumping to his feet and running up behind her. "Where are you going, my lady?" He fumbled with his mask, trying to put it back on his face.

"I'm going to spend the rest of the night in my chamber. Alone," she added as an afterthought, just so Adam wouldn't get any ideas of coming to see her. She was furious with him and needed to think about this situation in private.

"Nay, not your chamber, my lady," begged the squire. "What if I take you out to the stable instead? Or perhaps for a walk on the battlements."

"Why would I want to go anywhere with you?"

"Perhaps another dance, my lady. Just please don't go back to your chamber yet."

"Yet?" She raised a brow and studied his face. He held that silly mask up to his face and she could barely see his eyes. In one motion, she snatched the mask away from him and threw it to the floor. "Tell me what is going on. Where is Sir Adam and why don't you want me to go to my chamber?"

"No reason." His voice squeaked again.

"He told you to distract me, didn't he?" she asked, suddenly seeing things clearly. "He's in my chamber, isn't he?"

"I – I – I'm not sure where he is," said Bryce, not sounding at all convincing.

"I'm going to my chamber and if Sir Adam is in there, I'm going to wring his neck." She stormed off and Bryce followed. "If you don't turn around and stop following me, I'll have my grandmother do something horrible to you," she threatened as she continued to walk.

"Not Lady Barbara. That woman scares me," said the squire, stopping in his tracks.

Eva headed off to her solar without him tagging along, thinking that it wasn't that long ago when she was the one who scared men away. Bryce didn't seem frightened of her, just her grandmother, so she wondered if things had changed.

Eva didn't like the fact she was known to have frightened off men in the past. She wanted more than any young maiden to someday marry. But since the time her grandmother took her mother's place, Eva felt as if she didn't have a choice of her own. She always did what her grandmother told her. Now, she realized that she was turning into an old shrew like Lady Barbara. That didn't feel good at all.

Eva pushed open the door to her bedchamber, stopping in her tracks when she saw Adam standing at her desk. His back was to her and he was looking at something in his hand. Then she realized the lid to her chest was open and the missive was gone.

"Sir Adam!"

He turned on his heel, the missive dangling from his fingers. She realized that he was holding the parchment up to a candle, trying to read though it even though it was sealed in wax.

"Eva. What are you doing here?"

"Me?" She stormed into the room and slammed down the lid on the box. "Give it to me." Her hand shot out for the missive. He pulled it away and held it up over her head, out of her reach.

"You wrote this missive to the king, pretending to be your father, didn't you? Then you even sealed it in wax and used his signet ring to make it look like it came from him."

"You don't know what you're talking about."

"Don't I? I'm willing to bet this is a missive telling the king not to come here, just like the other missives he's been getting for the past six months." He used his thumb to break the seal, and scanned at the missive as she reached for it, trying to get it. He kept holding it higher above her head. "Just as I thought. You are forging messages from your father."

"I had to do it. It was for his own good," she tried to explain.

"His own good?" asked Adam, sounding sorely disappointed with her. "What is wrong with him?"

"I don't know what you mean."

"Don't play games with me, Eva. And don't think I didn't notice that he never uses his right hand. I'll bet that splint on his right leg has naught to do with bones being broken, but rather a ploy because he probably can't walk either, can he?"

"Stop it. You don't know what you're saying."

"His speech is always slurred although I realized that he hardly ever drinks, so it isn't from being well in his cups. Something happened to him and you are trying to keep everyone from knowing about it, aren't you?"

"He fell from a horse six months ago and broke his leg," Eva told him with tears in her eyes. "But afterwards we realized that he couldn't use his sword arm or his right leg. I cannot let the king know about it because if he does, he'll strip my father of his title and take away his castle and his lands forever."

ADAM DIDN'T KNOW what to say. Tears flowed from Eva's eyes, and he truly felt bad for her as well as the earl. But he was sent on a mission and to keep this information from the king would be treason.

"I'm sorry, Eva, but I can't ignore this now that I know the truth."

"What are you saying?" she asked. "You're not going to tell anyone are you?"

"The king needs to know about this. I have to tell him."

"*You* have to tell him? What does that mean? And how did you know about the other missives sent to the king?"

"He knows because he is the king's spy," said Lady Barbara, standing in the doorway.

"That's speculation and you can't prove it," said Adam, not wanting to admit in front of Eva that he'd been sent there on a mission for the king.

"And that's where you're wrong," snapped the woman. "I knew there was something deceitful about you, and I have the means to prove it." She looked down the hall and nodded. Bryce took a step forward with his head down.

"Bryce, you never could keep a secret," mumbled Adam, sorely disappointed.

"The old woman threatened to beat me with her cane the way she always hits the healer," exclaimed Bryce. "Plus, she threatened to have me thrown in the dungeon if I didn't tell her what she wanted to know." The boy gripped his mask in two hands, twisting it until it broke in two. "I'm sorry, Sir Adam. I had a little too much spiked wassail and wasn't thinking clearly. I told her everything."

"Everything? What do you mean, everything?" asked Eva with wide eyes.

"He used you, just as I told you he would," said her grandmother. "He seduced you with kisses and food just to learn our secrets and you stupidly fell for his games."

"Is that true?" asked Eva, looking at Adam as if she were

appalled. "You sent your squire to dance with me, so you really were using me and being deceitful."

"It is true that I am on a mission for the king to find out what is happening with the earl. But I assure you, I didn't seduce you," Adam told her.

"Oh, really?" She looked at him and raised an angry brow.

"Well, mayhap I did seduce you, but I assure you it wasn't just to get answers. I care for you, Lady Eva." He took a step toward her and she took one backward.

"Stay away from me and don't ever touch me again."

"You have to believe me when I tell you that I have feelings for you. You mean something to me. It wasn't so at first, but over the past sennight I – I think I have been falling in love with you."

"Hogwash," snapped her grandmother. "If that's true, then keep your mouth shut and don't say a word about this to the king."

"He has to tell him. It's his job," said Bryce. "After this mission, the king has promised to make Sir Adam a baron."

"Bryce!" Adam closed his eyes partially, knowing his squire's tongue was only going to make matters worse.

"So that's what this is all about?" asked Eva, looking at Adam as if she hated him right now. "You pretended to like me and give me everything I desired just so I would give you what you wanted?"

"Nay, that's not true," said Adam. "I gave you what you desired because I wanted to make you happy."

"You are naught but a liar," snapped Eva. "You hold the

power to ruin my father's life and take away everything from my family. How can you stand there and lie to my face? You only did all those nice things to get what you want. Well, get out of here and go tell the king whatever you have to, but don't ever show up on my doorstep again. If you do, I will throw you in my dungeon and have you beheaded."

"Eva, you don't understand. I have to tell the king. If I don't, it'll be treason."

"Then go!" she spat, holding out her finger and pointing at the door. "Go get your title of baron, and I hope you enjoy it. And take your squire with you."

"Eva," he said, stepping toward her, still holding on to the missive.

"Get out!" she shouted, picking up the wooden chest and throwing it at him.

Adam clenched his jaw, wanting to say so many things, but not being able to say a one. Instead, he clutched the missive tightly in his hand and stepped around her, making his way to the door. "Come, Squire," he said as he left the room. "We will not stay where we are not wanted."

CHAPTER 9

DANCING LADIES AND FORTUNETELLERS

*E*va sat at the dais the next day, eating some of the worst food she'd ever tasted in her life. It almost seemed like everyone was in sour spirits since she threw Adam and his squire out of the castle last night. The servants in the kitchen as well as the knights and every person in the castle asked where he was. She didn't say a word because she couldn't bring herself to tell them the truth.

Even her father had been asking for Adam. It was all too much and she could no longer live this way. She didn't want to lie anymore, so she told her father the whole truth. The earl had told her that it didn't matter what happened to him, but only that he wanted to see her happy.

Eva picked at the food on her trencher, not able to eat since she missed Adam so much. She'd tossed and turned all night, not able to sleep either. What had she done? Why hadn't she taken the time to talk things over with Adam?

Instead, she'd thrown him out and even threatened to have him imprisoned and beheaded. This was the old Eva rising back to the surface. She didn't like the old Eva anymore.

"You did the right thing," said her grandmother from next to her. Her father refused to come to the great hall saying things would never be the same without Adam. He had no desire to eat or play games anymore.

"I can't believe Adam deceived me like that," said Eva, feeling as if she wanted to cry. "I was falling in love with him, Grandmother."

"I warned you that he was no good. I could feel it in my bones. Now, because of him, we will lose everything. I wish you had never let him enter these castle walls. If I ever see his face again, I swear I will gouge out that man's eyes."

"Grandmother, please," said Eva, pushing away her trencher feeling that horrible knot in her stomach again.

"I am going to take your father some food and give the healer a break," said the woman, getting up and leaving the table.

Eva was about to get up and go to her chamber when the herald blew the straight trumpet and announced that a group of traveling gypsies had arrived to dance for them and tell their fortunes.

The music started and in came nine dancing ladies playing tambourines. They wore long, colorful clothes and veils covered their heads. Small bells were attached to the bottoms of their skirts so they jingled when they walked.

It didn't interest Eva, so she got up to leave. As she passed by the dancing ladies, the last one in the line grabbed her arm in a tight grip. She looked up, angry that the woman would touch her.

"I want to read your fortune," said the woman, turning her palm over.

"I don't think so." She tried to pull away but the woman had a strong grip. "Let go of me, or I'll call for my guards."

"Eva, don't do this to me."

"Adam?" She looked up into the gypsy's eyes to see that it, indeed, was him. "I thought I threw you out of here and warned you to never return."

"I had to talk to you, Eva. Please understand that I love you. I don't want to hurt you or your family."

"Then don't go to the king with the information," she challenged him.

"I don't have a choice. It's my job."

"Then don't come back here because I am not going to forgive you ever. I don't want anything to do with you ever again."

"Sir Adam, the old lady is coming down the stairs." Bryce hurried up to Adam wearing the same gypsy disguise and holding a tambourine. "I really think we ought to go."

"Grandmother," Eva called out, knowing that would scare the men off.

"Give me a chance to make it up to you, Eva," begged Adam. "I promise I'll find a way to make everything all right."

"What is it, Eva?" asked Lady Barbara, tapping her cane on the ground as she approached. "Are these gypsies giving you trouble? I'll call for the guards."

Eva stared into Adam's pleading eyes. Her head told her to let him rot in her dungeon, but her heart told her to give him another chance. "Nay, Grandmother, they are no trouble and were just leaving. They just wanted to read my palm and tell me that my future isn't as dim as it seems. I'll go with you to check on Father," she said, taking her grandmother's arm and leading her back up the stairs. When she got to the top and looked back down, Adam and his squire were gone.

CHAPTER 10

LEAPING LORDS

"*S*ir Adam, must we really go back into the castle?" complained Bryce the next morning. "I think it would be better to take your message back to the king. He's waiting for your report."

"I know he is, Squire, but I can't leave Cavendish before I make amends with Lady Eva." Adam sat on a rock and pulled the parti-colored leggings up to his waist. After paying the band of gypsies to show up at the castle yesterday, now they found a group of mummers that were headed to the castle. He paid them to let them join in their play. It was a silly play that involved lords leaping around in parti-colored clothes acting like fools, making up poems for the ladies of the castle. "This is the perfect way for us to get inside the castle and for me to make amends with Lady Eva."

"She's never going to forgive you, or haven't you noticed that she now hates your guts?" Bryce smeared some of the black paint over his face. "God's eyes, why do these mummers paint their faces?"

"Who knows, but it doesn't matter," said Adam, painting his face with an orange color. "But I would run naked through the castle if it would mean I'd get Lady Eva to like me again."

"You sound smitten with her, my lord."

"I am. I'm in love with her, Squire. And that is what makes this whole thing so awful. I have a duty to the king and I can't keep information from him. But I also don't want Lady Eva's family to suffer because of me."

"It wouldn't be because of you. She was the one deceiving the king."

"Aye, but I understand why she did it. She fears for her father. You know as well as I that a man who cannot fight and defend King Edward has no worth to him. Edward will, indeed, strip the earl of his title as well as take away his castle and lands."

"Aye, that he will," agreed Bryce.

"I have an idea, Squire. I think if I can get Lady Eva to go along with it, I might be able to still serve the king but, at the same time, save the earl from losing his castle and lands."

"What about his title?"

"That, I cannot save."

"What is your idea?"

"I am going to marry her right after the king makes me a baron. Then I'll convince Edward to give me Cavendish Castle and all the earl's lands. I'll let her father live with us, and I will even pay for the best healers to help him."

"What about the old lady? You're not going to let her stay, are you?" Bryce sounded very concerned.

"If this plan works, I'll not only let the old woman stay, but I'll kiss her under the kissing bough as well."

"Ugh, don't make me retch," said Bryce, wiping his hands on a rag.

* * *

"LADY EVA, THE MUMMERS HAVE ARRIVED," Sir Geoffrey, her steward, told her as a traveling troupe of performers in colored clothes with painted faces entered the great hall. "Shall I summon Lady Barbara and the earl?"

"Nay, Sir Geoffrey," answered Eva with a deep, sad sigh. "My father is sleeping late today as he's been very depressed ever since the departure of Sir Adam. And my grandmother is in the kitchen with the servants trying to figure out why the food tastes so bad lately."

"Well, then may I escort you into the great hall for the show, my lady?"

Eva nodded slightly. She didn't really want to see mummers, but as Lady of the Castle it was her duty to be present when outsiders arrived. She had been enjoying the Christmastide festivities when Adam was here but now she couldn't wait for them to end. When they did end, the king would arrive and then her life as she knew it would be over.

"Sit here in the front, my lady," said the steward, helping her get seated on the bench. "I'll bring you a goblet of wine to enjoy while you watch the show."

"Thank you, Steward," she said, not paying much attention as the music started and the colorful lords leapt into the room and up onto the trestle tables. Each of the men was dressed in parti-colored hose, half of the hose being one color and the other half was another. They wore tall hats that jutted out in all directions and had bells on the ends. They also had their faces painted in various colors and looked to her like naught but scary jesters.

"My lady, your eyes are like diamonds in the dark sky of a black velvet night," said one of the men, coming to her side. He knelt at her feet and held out a sprig of mistletoe. "Take it, Eva."

Her eyes snapped up to the man with the orange face and she almost cried out when she realized it was Adam. "How dare you keep sneaking back into the castle after I've told you to go." She got up and headed quickly across the hall and Adam followed.

"Please, Eva. I have an idea of how I can do my duty and your family won't lose everything in the process."

She stopped just outside of the great hall and folded her arms over her chest. "I'm listening."

"Marry me."

"Marry you?" she asked with a roll of her eyes. It was hard to take him seriously when he looked so ridiculous.

"Come here," he said, taking her away from the crowded room and over into the shadows in the corner. "I think it might work. Once I'm baron, I'll talk to the king and convince him to give me Cavendish Castle and your father's lands."

"What?" Shocked and appalled by his plan, she could barely believe her ears. "So you are going to use me again, marrying me only to gain what you want?"

"Nay, you don't understand. I'll be doing it to help you so you won't lose everything. As my wife, you'll still be Lady of Cavendish. Wouldn't that make you happy?"

"What about my father and grandmother?" she asked, still not buying his idea. "What will happen to them?"

"They can live here as well. I won't throw them out like you did to me."

"How noble of you," she grunted. "What about my father's title? Can you convince the king to let him keep the title of earl?"

"Nay, I'm afraid I'd never be able to that," he said with downcast eyes.

"Then forget it."

"Forget it?" He looked up as if she were addled. "Don't you understand what I'd be doing for you?"

"Don't do me any favors, because I don't want them." She turned and walked away.

"Stop being such a stubborn wench." His fingers closed around her arm and he twirled her around. "I love you, Eva, and I'll be damned if I'm going to just let you be thrown out of the castle and have to live like a pauper."

"Is that it?" she asked him. "So now you pity me and

that's why you're doing this? To save yourself from feeling guilty?"

"Dammit, Eva, how many times do I have to tell you I'm doing it because I love you and want you to be my wife?"

"It doesn't matter how many times you say it. I don't believe it."

"Then mayhap you'll believe this." He pulled her into his arms and kissed her hard and passionate, claiming her as his own. She melted in his embrace, feeling a tingling sensation running through her body. She did want Adam as her husband, but she was still angry with him for deceiving her. Plus, she didn't believe he could do all the things he said he would do. The king was a stubborn and powerful man and it was hard to influence him. Her father had always told her that through the years.

"Adam, the troupe is leaving," said another of the players with a black face that sounded like Bryce.

"Think about it," said Adam, releasing her. "And the next time I show up, I want your answer."

As much as it hurt her, she knew what her answer had to be. "I won't marry you, so please stop asking. I don't believe you can talk the king into the things you so confidently think you can get him to agree to. And I cannot be married to a man who was the one responsible for my father losing his title as well as his castle, his lands, and also his pride."

"Is that the way you really feel?" he asked her.

"It is."

"Then if you don't trust and believe me, I suppose there is no reason for me to return."

"I suppose not." She still vibrated from his kiss, and focused on the ground as she held her arms around her. She couldn't look into his eyes because then he would see how much she really wanted him.

"Look at me when you say you don't want me, Eva." He reached out and lifted her chin with his hand. "Look me in the eye and tell me you don't love me and that you want me to leave forever. Do that, and I will go and never bother you again."

"I don't love you, and I want you to go," she said, about choking on the words because she didn't really mean them. But this is what she had to do. Her grandmother would never let her marry Adam, and her father would be nothing but a broken man if his title were taken from him. She couldn't marry Adam when her family was going to have to pay for his actions.

"Goodbye, Eva," he said softly, making her want to cry. He left immediately with his squire. Eva stood there watching, not able to call him back even though she wanted to be his wife more than anything in the world. She had made a decision that she thought her grandmother would want her to make. Her decision was in the best interests of her father, she told herself. Adam was only using her to get what he wanted, wasn't he? Suddenly, she was no longer sure.

CHAPTER 11

PIPERS AND DRUMMERS

Two days had passed and Eva didn't see Adam again. When the troupe of pipers showed up at her doorstep yesterday playing bagpipes and wearing plaids, she was sure one of them was Adam. But alas, none of them were.

And today a group of traveling musicians put on a show playing drums. Her head had been about to split open as she went from one drummer to another looking into each of their eyes hoping one of them was Adam. None of them were.

Tomorrow was the Epiphany and also the day the king was to arrive at her doorstep. Since Adam had taken her missive and gone to the king with all her family's secrets, there was no hope that the king wouldn't show up.

With the drummers gone now, she sat at the fire watching the remains of the Yule log burning away. The cage with the doves named Adam and Eve sat on the table next to her. The birds chirped happily and seemed to be in love, not worried about the future or the past. If only she could be as carefree. The turtle doves were a gift from Adam and she would cherish them always.

"Lady Eva," said her steward, coming to her side. "Should I pull the rest of the Yule log out of the fire since it is almost consumed? It is custom to always save a piece for the next year to bring good luck."

"Nay," she said, staring into the flames, trying to forget about all her trouble. "Let it burn. There is no good luck coming to this family ever again. Sir Geoffrey, I haven't told anyone, but now I'm going to tell you something that I should have mentioned long ago."

"My lady? What is it?"

"I've been keeping you from speaking with my father for the past six months because I didn't want you to know that he can no longer use his sword arm. His leg is no longer broken, but I have the healer keep the splint on it because he cannot use his right leg either."

"I know, my lady. I've known for a long time and so has everyone else in the castle," Geoffrey told her.

"You do?" she asked, surprised. "And yet you didn't say a word?"

"Nay, my lady. It wasn't my position to question your ways. It is no secret that the earl's speech is slurred although he is not drunk. Everyone realizes his condition but we ignore it because we honor and respect the man and don't want him to be reminded that he may never again be the strong warrior he used to be."

Tears filled Eva's eyes. "Now I feel like the biggest fool of all. In trying to protect my father and his holdings, I have deceived not only you and everyone in this castle but also the king."

"The king?" asked Sir Geoffrey.

"Yes. I wrote missives to the king to ward him off, pretending they were coming from my father."

"I see." The knight remained quiet for a moment and then looked up. "May I speak freely, my lady?"

"Please do."

"Is this part of the reason why Sir Adam left?"

"It is. He discovered my secrets. He is the king's spy."

"A spy?"

"Aye. He used me to get what he wanted and now he wants to marry me so my family can hold on to Cavendish Castle as well as my family's lands."

"Then why don't you do it, Eva?" came her father's voice from behind her. Eva turned to see her grandmother standing there holding on to the back of her father's wheeled chair. She must have brought him into the room without Eva realizing it since she was so lost in deep thought.

"Father," she said, jumping up and running to his side. "What are you saying?"

"I may be only half a man but I still have eyes," he told her. "I saw the way you and Sir Adam looked at each other. I like the man. He makes me laugh."

"Not to mention he is the best cook we've had at this

castle since your mother passed away," added Lady Barbara.

"Grandmother?" Eva looked at the old woman in surprise. "Are you saying you agree with Father that I should marry Sir Adam?"

"If it'll make you happy and your father wants you to, then who am I to object?" answered Lady Barbara with a sigh.

"Sir Adam wants to marry me," she told them excitedly. "He was promised the title of baron if he brought the king information about you, Father."

"I see." He glared at Lady Barbara. "I didn't know you two were writing missives to the king in my name, and although I thank you for trying to protect me, I am not happy about all the deception." He talked slowly and his speech was still slurred, but he seemed to be trying hard to control it.

"So you would rather have had the king know about your accident and strip you of your title and take away your castle and lands because of it?" asked Eva.

"Daughter, I have lived a good life. And while no man wants to live as half a man, not able to defend his family or king, accidents do happen. If it is my destiny to live this way, then so be it."

"Father, how can you say that?" asked Eva, tears dripping down her cheeks. "You are a good man and deserve all these things."

"So is Sir Adam. You should marry him, Daughter. He

will protect you and take care of you. That is something I will never be able to do again."

"I love you, Father." Eva hugged the man and gave him a kiss on his cheek.

"Do you love Sir Adam?" asked her father.

"I do. I love Adam and want to be his wife."

"Then, mayhap before I am stripped of my title, I will betroth you to him."

"Nay," she said with a shake of her head. "I have already told him I don't love him and that I don't want to be his wife. It is too late."

"It's never too late," said her father. "Have faith, my dear."

"Mince cakes?" asked a servant girl holding a tray in front of Eva.

"Nay," she said, sniffing and wiping a tear from her eyes. "Wait, I would like one," she decided, holding it up and taking a bite. And, once again, she made the wish for her father's health to return and, this time, to be Sir Adam's wife.

CHAPTER 12

THE ARRIVAL OF A KING

Twelfth Night was over and the Epiphany had come. This was the day that the Magi arrived to see the baby Jesus, a long, long time ago.

Eva waited at the door of the keep nervously, waiting for one king, not three, although she wished for no kings on this day.

King Edward's procession entered through her front gate. This was the day when her life would change forever. Taking a deep breath and releasing it, she walked alongside Sir Geoffrey, hurrying across the courtyard to greet Edward and his wife, Queen Philippa.

Her father waited with her grandmother inside the great hall. The servants in the kitchen had been cooking since before the rise of the sun, trying to prepare something suitable to serve a king in case he should arrive at their door. She felt so nervous that her knees knocked together whenever she stood still.

"The King and Queen of England," announced the herald. The courtyard filled quickly with knights and nobles as well as servants as everyone gathered around to greet their ruler.

"Your Majesty," said Eva, holding on to Sir Geoffrey's arm and curtseying to the king as he dismounted. The king helped his wife from her horse and they both strolled over to her. Dressed in rich clothes with crowns on their heads and rings on their fingers, Eva would have marveled at the sight of their noble, elaborate entourage if she hadn't been dreading it so much.

"Lady Eva, I don't see your father," said Edward, looking over the heads of the onlookers. "I would think he would be here to greet me." Edward's red hair and long beard made him look even more majestic. And Queen Philippa at his side looked so beautiful that it took her breath away. Now Eva felt even lower than she had before, because she was naught but a liar looking straight into the eyes of those she had deceived.

"My king," she said, looking up to Edward in question. Why would he ask such a thing? "I'm sure Sir Adam has told you that my father had an accident and can no longer use his sword arm or even walk since he lost the use of one leg."

By the surprised look on the king's face, she realized he knew none of this. "Sir Adam told me nothing of the sort," said Edward, glancing over to his wife. "But had he given me the information, he would have been made baron."

"What are you saying?" asked Eva, feeling her heart

beating rapidly against her ribs. "Isn't Sir Adam one of your . . . spies?"

"He used to be," answered the king. "And he was damned good at his job. But when he failed to complete his last mission, I was severely disappointed in him. I was willing to give him one last chance to earn the chance of becoming a baron, but he turned me down."

"He did?" asked Eva, unable to believe her ears. Only a fool would turn down the chance of becoming a baron.

"Aye, he turned me down, even though he'd wanted the title for a very long time. I don't understand why, and he didn't explain. However, it was then that he asked for his leave from his position. It sounded like it was what he really wanted, so I granted him the right to go his own way."

"He left?" she asked. "Where did he go?"

"I do not know, Lady Eva. All I know is that to turn down the chance of becoming a baron is the only stupid move the man has ever made."

"My dear, it is good to see you again," said Queen Philippa, breaking into the conversation. "Now, if you'll kindly escort us inside, I'd like a warm cup of mead and to get out of the cold."

"Of course, my queen," she said, blindly, curtseying and escorting the sovereigns into the castle. She found it hard to believe that Adam had never told the king about her missives or about her father's condition. He must truly have loved her, she realized, to keep her family's secret and turn down the chance of becoming a baron as well. Now, she worried for him since, as he said, keeping information from the king could very well be considered treason.

"Earl Cavendish," said the king as soon as they entered the keep. "I hear you've had an accident and are no longer able to serve me."

"Aye," said her father, not saying anything more.

"Well, I am sorry to hear it. And I am also sorry to have to tell you that I cannot allow you to keep your title. Neither can I allow you to keep the castle or your lands."

"It's all right, my king," said the earl, about breaking Eva's heart. "It was an honor to serve you all these years, and I would do the same if I were in your position." His words were still slurred, but not as much as usual. Eva figured her father was trying his best to keep up appearances in front of the king. "Your Majesty, before you strip me of my title, I have but one request."

"What is it?" asked the king, fingering his beard.

"I ask that you allow me to betroth my daughter to the knight, Sir Adam de Ware."

"Sir Adam?" the queen asked, looking up in surprise.

"Is this something that Sir Adam wants as well?" asked Edward.

"I am sure he does," answered the earl, even though Eva could no longer believe it. "He has actually asked my daughter to marry him."

"Then it's done," said Edward with a flick of his wrist. "Now, bring on the food. We have had a long journey and the queen and I are famished."

"Steward, tell the servants to bring the food at once,"

said Eva quickly, feeling that knot in her stomach return. She didn't want the king's last impression of her family to be the horrible-tasting food that they were about to serve him.

To her surprise, a procession of servants came marching from the kitchen, each of them carrying one dish after another that looked and smelled amazing. She could only watch with her mouth hanging open, wondering how the servants managed to pull this off. And when the meal started and she tasted the food, she was in shock. It tasted as good as the food prepared by Sir Adam.

"This is the best food I've ever tasted," said the king, digging into one course after another as if he couldn't get enough.

"I agree," said the queen, dabbing her mouth with a cloth. "It tastes an awful lot like some of the meals Sir Adam used to cook for us before he left the castle."

"Sir Adam used to cook? For you?" asked Eva in surprise.

"Oh, he never let anyone know about it, since it isn't considered an acceptable action from a knight," said Philippa with a giggle. "It was our secret."

"And it was a secret worth keeping," remarked Edward. "I will miss the man's cooking. However, now that I've tasted food equally as delicious, I might steal your cook instead. It is hard to believe there is another that matches the skills of Sir Adam in the kitchen. Who cooks for you, Lady Eva?"

"Well, I –" Eva stopped in midsentence when she saw

Adam, dressed in his chain mail tunic and wearing his leather arm guards, emerge from the kitchen carrying a tray with a seed cake on top.

"Your Majesties," said Adam, bowing to the king and queen. "Earl. Lady Barbara. Lady Eva." His eyes flashed over to each of them as he greeted them one by one. When he looked at her, his gaze lingered, and she felt her heart skip a beat.

"Adam," she said under her breath, wanting to apologize for the horrible way she'd treated him the last time they were together.

"De Ware, what the hell are you doing here?" asked the king.

"I'm here as Lady Eva's cook. And knight," added Adam, with a bow of his head. "That is, if she'll have me."

"Adam," whispered Eva, her bottom lip trembling as he handed her a piece of seed cake.

"For you, my lady," he told her in his charming manner. Her heart melted. She had missed his smile.

"I don't think I can eat at a time like this," she muttered, pushing the cake away.

"Take a bite," he said with a nod of his head, pushing the piece of cake back toward her. "But I must warn you to be careful."

"Careful?" she asked, suddenly intrigued. "Is there something inside this cake that I don't know about?" It was custom on the Feast of the Magi to serve a cake with a bean, a coin, or a ring served inside it. Whoever got the bean was king for the day. The person who found the coin would be wealthy and the ring meant that person would be married soon.

"There is only one way to find out," he answered.

Curiously, Eva picked up the piece of cake and took a bite. When she did, she felt something made of metal in her mouth. She pulled it out, and held it in her palm.

"It's a ring," she announced, looking at Adam and then over to her father.

"The king stripped me of my title, castle and lands," the earl told Adam. "But he agreed to let me betroth my daughter to you."

"I would like that," said Adam.

"And so would I." Eva cried, tears dripping down her cheeks. "I want to marry you, Sir Adam. However, I cannot marry you without first telling the king the truth about those missives." Eva spoke the truth, fearing for her life yet at the same time not wanting to start a new life while harboring lies.

"Lady Eva," said the king, licking his fingers as he spoke. "If you are talking about the fact you wrote those missives and not your father, I already know. Sir Adam told me months ago his suspicions that a woman was writing the messages and not the earl. We deciphered it was either you or your grandmother."

"Months ago?" she asked, looking over to Adam.

"Aye," answered Adam. "I knew you were probably the one forging the missives before I ever set foot into Cavendish Castle. I could tell by your writing and your choice of words that it wasn't coming from a man. What we didn't know was why the earl was letting you do it." Adam turned and addressed the king next. "Your Majesty, I have kept the information of the earl's condition from you and, for that, I will take any punishment that you see fit. But before you do, I need to tell you that I love Lady Eva and the reason I didn't tell you was because I didn't want her and her family to end up living as paupers."

"Aye," said the king, stroking his beard in thought. "Keeping information from me could be considered treason."

"Oh, please, don't punish him," begged Eva. "Punish me instead. I never should have asked him not to tell you about it in the first place. I only did it because I was afraid of my father losing everything he has worked so hard to attain in his life. The accident never should have happened to such a wonderful man, and my heart breaks to see him in this condition."

"I see," said the king. "It is most unfortunate. Sir Adam, I understand your dilemma, and that you love Lady Eva, but that is still no excuse. You have done me wrong, and I am afraid I will have to punish you in some way."

"But he didn't give you a missive I wrote," said Eva. "If he really wanted to keep the information from you, wouldn't he have given you the missive saying not to come to Cavendish at all?"

"Eva, the king already knew you were writing the missives, so there was no need to give it to him," explained Adam.

"But you didn't stop him from coming here, Adam. Yet,

you knew full well that he would discover my father's condition as soon as he arrived."

"I did," admitted Adam. "I couldn't betray my king, yet I couldn't betray you either, Eva. I figured this was the best way to inadvertently complete my mission, yet at the same time show you how much you mean to me as well. By letting the king arrive in Cavendish, I have given him the chance to learn the truth about your father. And by not giving him your missive, I never came out and told him what I'd learned."

"That's true," her father spoke up. "He gave up the chance of being a baron because of his love for you, Eva."

"Aye, you did," she said, feeling her heart breaking even more.

"Enough! I will have no sad faces today," Edward commanded, putting another piece of food into his mouth. "De Ware, as far as I'm concerned, you completed your last mission for me. Even if it wasn't what I expected."

"Your Majesty?" asked Adam. "What are you saying?"

"I'm saying, if you are going to marry the daughter of an earl then you will need a better title than just Sir."

"Daughter of an earl?" asked Adam, cocking his head. "Didn't you just say the earl no longer holds his title?"

"Let me finish." Edward took a swig of ale and smacked his lips together, still enjoying the food. "I've decided I am going to make you a baron after all."

"You are?" Adam looked confused and too stunned to even thank him.

"That's right." Edward turned to talk to Eva's father

next. "Earl Cavendish, you can keep your title since you were always one of my favorites and in the past have risked your life to protect me, fighting at my side. I will even pardon your mother and daughter since I know they were only trying to help you. But because of your condition and the fact you can no longer fight or defend anyone, I am giving your castle and lands to Baron de Ware."

"That sounds good by me," said Eva's father, making Eva's heart soar by the way he was smiling again.

"Thank you, Your Majesty," said Adam, snapping out of his daze. "I will never even consider withholding information from you again."

"You'd better not, de Ware, or there will be hell to pay."

"You won't be sorry," said Adam. "I promise you that. I will hold my position as baron with pride and honor every day of my life."

"What about me?" asked Lady Barbara. "Where will my son and I live now that the castle is gone?"

"You'll stay right here at Cavendish where you belong," answered Adam, walking up to the dais to gather Eva into his arms. "After all, my wife will want her family close and that's how it'll stay. Lady Barbara will stay at Cavendish, just as well as my squire. Isn't that right, Bryce?" Adam called out to his squire who was across the hall.

"Aye, my lord," said Bryce with a gulp, making everyone laugh since he still feared the old woman and her cane.

"Then there is just the issue of your punishment, Sir Adam." King Edward scooped more food atop his trencher.

"I am ready for the verdict, Your Majesty," Adam said, bowing his head.

Eva gripped Adam's hand tightly, fearing that the punishment might be something horrible like being locked in the dungeon, or put up on display tied to a stake atop the battlements. Her hand went to her shoulder that had been scarred by the guard's whip. With Adam's comfrey salve, she was almost healed. But what if the king ordered Adam to be whipped? She feared for his safety and what might happen to him.

"I have made my decision," announced Edward. "Baron Adam de Ware, your punishment will be that you come to my castle once a week and work in my kitchen cooking delicious food like this for my wife and me."

"Cook?" asked Lady Barbara in surprise. "You want him to cook for you as his punishment? That's all?"

Edward glared at Lady Barbara from the sides of his eyes. "Did you want me to convict you as well, Lady Barbara? Because if you don't think his punishment is enough, I can punish you as well for your part in all this deceit."

"Nay, not all, Your Majesty," said Lady Barbara, looking at the ground.

"My king, I am honored that you like my food," said Adam. "However, cooking is not a punishment to me, as I truly enjoy it."

"Mayhap it isn't," said Edward. "However, not having your food at my castle will be a punishment to me. So that is my decision."

"Then I accept," said Adam, laughing, pulling Eva to his chest in a hug. She looked up to see him holding something over her head.

"What are you doing?" she asked with a giggle.

"I am holding a sprig of mistletoe above your head so you will kiss me," he told her.

"You don't need that," she said, kissing the man she loved who was about to become her husband. "After all, weren't you the one who told me I was your Mistletoe?"

"Aye, and I am your Chain Mail," said Adam, kissing her passionately in front of everyone.

Eva could barely wait to be his wife.

And so the Twelve Days of Christmas that had started out rocky, ended in a very joyful celebration for everyone involved. Two people were brought together in marriage not long afterwards with a celebration that included some of the best food known to the land.

With Adam and Eva's wedding came a new tradition. Every year at Christmastide, a new kissing bough constructed by the couple hung over the dais, right above the Lord and Lady of the Castle's chairs. Adam and Eva kissed under it often, looking up to the ornate kissing bough above their heads that was constructed from none other than *Mistletoe and Chain Mail*.

FROM THE AUTHOR

I hope you enjoyed Adam and Eva's story and will take a moment to leave a review for me.

I am so excited about my new *Holiday Knights* series that will include many holidays and the extensive research woven into the stories to let you experience the traditions and customs of medieval times.

One of the things I was amazed to learn while researching this book was the origin of piggy banks. Back in medieval times, metal was expensive, so an orange clay called pygg was used for making jars and vessels. On St. Stephen's Day, the lord would give little clay pots with slits in the top to his servants, putting a penny in each one. The poor could save their pennies in this jar, having to break it open in order to retrieve the money. (Hence, the first piggy banks.) Now, how it turned into a pig was all by accident. Hundreds of years later, someone got the order to make pyggs. But he thought he was supposed to create pigs instead. It was a funny mistake and people liked the idea of saving money in a jar shaped like a pig. Therefore, pygg jars turned into piggy banks instead.

I find things like this quite interesting and hope to bring about more knowledge of the medieval ages through this series. I loved the play on the *Twelve Days of Christmas*, and learned that the calling birds from the song were really collie birds, or blackbirds. They really did have live blackbirds pop out of a pie back then as a novelty – not to eat. However, it is to my understanding that the crust of the pie was thick and domed and cooked beforehand and that the birds were placed into the piecrust after it cooled. Remember the rhyme about four and twenty blackbirds baked in a pie? Well, there you go.

The books in this series will be sweet and clean romance novellas. If you prefer a little spice in your stories or would like to read full-length novels instead, please visit my website to find out more about my other books.

Watch for more *Holiday Knights* coming soon.

Elizabeth Rose

ABOUT ELIZABETH

Elizabeth Rose is a multi-published, bestselling author, writing medieval, historical, contemporary, paranormal, and western romance. She is an amazon all-star and an award-nominee. Her books are available as Ebooks, paperback, and audiobooks as well.

Her favorite characters in her works include dark, dangerous and tortured heroes, and feisty, independent heroines who know how to wield a sword. She loves writing 14th century medieval novels, and is well-known for her many series.

Her twelve-book small town contemporary series, Tarnished Saints, was inspired by incidents in her own life.

After being traditionally published, she started self-publishing, creating her own covers and book-trailers on a dare from her two sons.

Elizabeth is a born storyteller and passionate about sharing her works with her readers.

Please be sure to visit her website at **Elizabethrosenovels.com** to read excerpts from any of her novels and get sneak peeks at covers of upcoming books. You can follow her on **Twitter, Facebook**, **Goodreads** or **BookBub.**

ALSO BY ELIZABETH ROSE

Medieval

Legendary Bastards of the Crown Series

Seasons of Fortitude Series

Secrets of the Heart Series

Legacy of the Blade Series

Daughters of the Dagger Series

MadMan MacKeefe Series

Barons of the Cinque Ports Series

Second in Command Series

Holiday Knights Series

Highland Chronicles Series

Medieval/Paranormal

Elemental Magick Series

Greek Myth Fantasy Series

Tangled Tales Series

Contemporary

Tarnished Saints Series

Working Man Series

<u>Western</u>

Cowboys of the Old West Series

And more!

Please visit http://elizabethrosenovels.com

Elizabeth Rose

CPSIA information can be obtained
at www.ICGtesting.com
Printed in the USA
LVHW031516190922
728748LV00003B/620

9 781731 227164